standing

on

richards

Also by George Bowering

FICTION

Diamondback Dog

Piccolo Mondo

Parents from Space

Shoot!

Harry's Fragments

Caprice

Burning Water

A Short Sad Book

NON-FICTION

Bowering's B.C.

Egotists and Autocrats

Stone Country

POETRY

Blonds on Bikes

Urban Snow

Rocky Mountain Foot

The Gangs of Kosmos

standing

on

richards

GEORGE BOWERING

VIKING
CANADA

VIKING CANADA

Penguin Group (Canada), a division of Pearson Penguin Canada Inc.,
10 Alcorn Avenue, Toronto, Ontario M4V 3B2

Penguin Group (U.K.), 80 Strand, London WC2R 0RL, England
Penguin Group (U.S.), 375 Hudson Street, New York, New York 10014, U.S.A.
Penguin Group (Australia) Inc., 250 Camberwell Road, Camberwell, Victoria 3124,
Australia
Penguin Group (Ireland), 25 St. Stephen's Green, Dublin 2, Ireland
Penguin Books India (P) Ltd, 11, Community Centre, Panchsheel Park,
New Delhi – 110 017, India
Penguin Group (NZ), cnr Airborne and Rosedale Roads, Albany, Auckland 1310,
New Zealand
Penguin Books (South Africa) (Pty) Ltd, 24 Sturdee Avenue, Rosebank 2196, South Africa

Penguin Group, Registered Offices: 80 Strand, London WC2R 0RL, England

First published 2004

1 2 3 4 5 6 7 8 9 10   (RRD)

Manufactured in the United States of America.

NATIONAL LIBRARY OF CANADA CATALOGUING IN PUBLICATION

Bowering, George, 1935–
Standing on Richards / George Bowering.

ISBN 0-670-04454-7

I. Title.

PS8503.O875S73   2004   C813'.54   C2004-900622-3

Visit the Penguin Group (Canada) website at **www.penguin.ca**

*   *   *

This collection is for Mike and Carol Matthews

contents

introduction

Longing for the Short

I don't know what has happened to the short story. When I was a kid, it was probably the most often encountered of all literary forms. The literary magazines carried stories, of course. So did the glossy magazines, the weeklies, and monthlies. Most of those magazines have gone now, replaced by specialty magazines (tattoos, motorcycles, fashion) and the dumbed-down picture mags about television stars and children's music makers. The pulps were made for short stories, but the pulps are gone, even the high quality pulps. I pity the younger generations who do not know the pulps.

That leaves the literary magazines. Most people don't even know that they exist. Their print runs are shorter than any short story. Still, they are about it as far as publication of short stories goes. How are they going to keep up? In Canada everyone is a story writer. In Canada all our novelists and poets are also short-story writers. All but Robert Kroestch and Michael Ondaatje—and wouldn't you like to see what they could do in the form?

The hotshot kids pouring out of our creative-writing mills are as capable as can be in the making of regulation short

ix

stories. They know all the moves, and they get agents before they get their degrees. They publish their first novels and then they publish their first books of stories. Or the other way round. We have a few anthologies every year, but for every short story that is published this year, there were probably fifty in 1938. Writers such as F. Scott Fitzgerald didn't bother collecting most of their magazine stories into books.

So with such a small market, why would anyone want to write short stories, even the book of linked stories that some professors have mistakenly called a peculiarly Canadian form? Well, a lot of writers just cannot get their heads into the marketplace. Otherwise they would be turning out hockey books and children's stories about funny body noises.

Put it more specifically: why would *I* want to write short stories when I could be writing a non-fiction book about baseball or prime ministers, for example? Well, for one thing, I write a lot fewer short stories than I would like to. I have an idea notebook that contains a lot of aging ideas for stories, and every few days I have an idea that doesn't even make it into my idea notebook. And sometimes an idea just does not work when one finally gets round to trying it out—such as my story about a guy who wants to find his way out of a building with rooms made out of Ezra Pound's cantos.

My first novel, thanks be to God that it was never published, was of course all about a bright sensitive lad something like the author, and his years till he came to writing his first novel. My earliest stories were sentimentalized tales of masculine travails and dangers. Then some dope said that one should write what one knows. So my earliest published stories tend to be about a lad's life in a small town in orchard country. In the middle of my life I found myself wandering in a dark orchard, and came to realize that my only way out was to quit asking myself this question: "what was it really like to be a high school kid in love?" I started asking myself this question, instead: "I wonder whether you can get away with having a guy break the Ten Commandments, in order?" In my most recent stories there's a kind of confident relating of little incidences of strangers meeting or making slight human connections. How nice not to have to remember what a certain hillside looked like.

Well, it's all writing. And the nicest thing about writing is feeling the sentence form while you are handwriting or typing. Sometimes when you are feeling a sentence form, you know that it is going to be one of a thousand, but other times you know that there are going to be maybe a hundred. You probably love this sentence most. You feel them all, though, and you will return to the big building job of a novel or the history book that you know is really a novel. There are some writers who start with stories and then begin making novels and never come back to the shorter form. I will always, I think, want to come back, if only to try out something I hadn't thought of earlier.

Anyway, having a collection of short stories published makes me feel young again. That's kind of contradictory, given the fact that it is partly made of stories from earlier volumes. Maybe what I mean is that I feel like an upcoming Canadian writer with more stories to tell. Okay, stories to invent.

STANDING ON RICHARDS

Richards Street in downtown Vancouver is pretty interesting or pretty boring, depending on your point of view. Of all the people standing on corners along Richards Street, I am probably the only one who knows that it was named after Captain George Harry Richards, the nineteenth-century surveyor who gave False Creek its name.

Try it. Go up to one of the girls on the corner of Richards and, say, Nelson and ask, "Hey, did you know that this street was named after the nineteenth-century surveyor who gave False Creek its name?"

"Oh, yeah, like I really give a shit about that." That's what she'll say.

Most nights I stand on the corner of Richards and Helmcken. Helmcken, by the way, was a Hudson's Bay Company doctor who made a lot of money on real estate around Victoria in the late nineteenth century. He was cosy with the Americans.

1

I don't look like anyone else standing on corners along Richards. You go down to Richards and Nelson, and you get your tall young women in high heels. In the summer you can see the cheeks of their asses. In the winter they are nearly freezing because they might have winter coats, but they leave them open so guys in slowly cruising cars can see their long legs. An awful lot of them are blondes of one sort or another, because the Asian businessmen and tourists don't come all the way over here for women with dark hair.

I like Danielle. She has the darkest hair you ever saw, and she doesn't care. She's got eyes that could give a Japanese volleyball coach a heart attack. She's also got a PhD in anthropology. But when it came to selling, she decided to sell her body. I have nothing against her body.

That's a witticism.

I have nothing against her decision. As far as I can see, she's the only girl on Richards who had to make that choice.

A couple blocks in the other direction you'll see the boys and the young men trying to look like boys, around Richards and whatever that street is on the other side of Davie. If you want to be one of those boys, you have to be skinny. You have to look as if you could get hurt easily, and you have to know what to wear, no T-shirts with designer names on them, no No Fear, no Club Monaco. You don't want to be wearing a baseball cap backward. A nice clean pair of tans and a white shirt with some buttons undone will do the trick. You have to look as if you've done this before, just to be safe, and you have to look as if you haven't been doing this for long. There aren't any real stores or cafes down there past Davie, so you stand out like a sore you know what.

Usually I am the only person standing on the corner of Richards and Helmcken. Hardly anyone pronounces that name right. It is something like "Helmakin." Or it was when it was still attached to John S. Helmcken, the first doctor to show up in Victoria, in 1850. He married one of Governor Douglas's daughters and started buying up real estate. Doctors have been doing something like that ever since, except maybe the doctors who try to take care of the less lucky people standing on corners along Richards Street.

So I was going to tell you that I look somewhat different from the other people standing on corners along Richards. You won't see my bare legs, that's for certain, and I do not look in any way like a boy. I guess I look like a college professor from about twenty years ago. I'm wearing brown shoes, no sign of recent polishing, laces not as long as they used to be. Gabardine slacks, either dark brown or grey, I'm not sure. A light blue long-sleeve shirt with an ink stain at the bottom of the pocket and a tie with stripes on a slant. One of those generic old school ties, somewhat wider than the ties I see salesmen wearing these days. Bifocal glasses that have frames halfway between round and square. And a genuine Harris tweed jacket.

Let me explain why I said "genuine." You see, first of all, a lot of people think that tweeds are called tweeds because they are woven in the Tweed Valley. Well, some of them are woven in the Tweed Valley, but that is not how we got the word "tweed." Tweeds are made from varieties of the old twill weave, and the old Scottish word for twill is "tweel." In 1826 some clerk in London made an understandable mistake, writing "tweed" instead of "tweel," and it was not long until our jackets were called tweeds, even in Scotland.

So what about Harris? Well, if you go across The Minch from the top of mainland Scotland, you will come to the biggest island in the Outer Hebrides. Stornaway Castle is up there, you may remember. Well, really it is all one island called Lewis Island, but the locals always refer to two islands, Lewis and Harris. No one knows why, but it may be because Lewis is a lot hillier, or mountainous, as they say over there. In any case, if someone had not started the Harris tweel cottage industry, they would have had to get by on fishing, and you know how unlikely that has become over the years.

So that's why I said "genuine." Harris tweeds are the most northerly tweeds, so the sheep they get the wool from have the thickest and toughest texture. That's my theory, anyway. If you are interested in a tweed jacket, have a good look at the label. Look for the word "genuine."

I said that I look like a professor from about twenty years ago. In fact I *was* a professor twenty years ago. I was a professor *five* years ago, professor of English. I was one of those strange ducks who kept reading outside my field of expertise. In fact, most people in my field of expertise, Nineteenth-Century American Literature, knew a lot more about the recent work in the field than I did. I didn't want to stop reading Latin poetry and Japanese novels and provincial history, so I sort of fell behind in the latest theory about criticism of nineteenth-century American prose and/or poetry. Every time I started to read some of the latest theory about criticism in my field of expertise, I would run into the word "hegemonic" or the word "template." So I would put the paper aside and pick up Plutarch.

But that is not the real reason I quit being a professor. Not the only one, anyway. I quit because I was finding it difficult to locate anyone who wanted to know anything about literature. Once in a while I would have to supervise a graduate student who was interested in hegemonic templates in recent criticism of W. D. Howells, and I would encourage that young person to read *The Atlantic Monthly* from 1871 through 1881. But I was always tabbed to do more than my share of first-year English classes. An Introduction to English Fiction—that sort of thing.

Maybe there's something wrong with me. I still get all excited when I read an author I have never bothered with before, someone like, say, Mrs. Chapone. Or when I find a new book about Fort Simpson and the Christian missionaries along the northern coast.

So you can imagine how I felt when September would slide into October, and it would become apparent that the young-sters in their backward caps and Club Monaco sweatshirts didn't particularly want to learn anything. In fact, more and more of them let it be known that once they had paid their tuition money they thought it was an imposition to make them read anything as well.

So I quit.

I wanted to see whether there was someplace where I could sell my mind to someone who wanted to buy it.

I told this story to Danielle. She told me that she understood perfectly. She probably did. She never told me whether
she had quit a professor job or whether she had just got a PhD
for the fun of it and didn't want to drive a cab.

You might say, Who would stop their car and haggle over
price with a guy in a tweed jacket who wants to sell his mind
on Richards Street? I know I did. But I thought that I would
give it a try. If that didn't work, there must be lots of other
ways of selling your mind. Well, that's what I had been doing
for twenty years at the university on the hill.

In recent years the university had acquired some high-rise
space for a campus extension downtown, just off the financial
district. Twenty-five tired students and I used to sit in a room
with sealed windows every Tuesday night, two hours and a
cigarette break and two more hours, not a coffee shop within
walking distance because the businessmen were all at home
drinking vodka. Then I would walk up Howe Street, turn right
on Georgia, turn right into a lane, and get into my professor
car. Head home, have a last coffee, and lie in bed, trying to
remember what I had to teach in the morning.

When you turned right at Georgia Street in those times, you
walked past a number of tall young prostitutes trying to look
upscale. One night after four hours of trying to get tired
students interested in reading Henry James, I was walking past
the genteel windows in front of the Georgia Hotel, when a
good-looking young woman with glowing dark brown skin
spoke to me.

"Would you like some company?"

She sounded cheerful.

"No, thanks. I'm going to go home and read," I said, still walking.

"I'll read to you," she called out as I turned in at the lane.

I did not change my pace, but I imagined, not for the last time, bringing that pleasant woman home to read to me. In a negligee, I guess. Say, hanging open in the front. One glowing breast peeking out, let's say.

So one sunny day in June I took along my old flaked briefcase and stood on the corner of Richards and Helmcken. I had books in the briefcase, and the first thing I did was to set the briefcase down and take out Margaret Ormsby's *British Columbia: A History* and start reading. I would read a paragraph and then scan the windshields of slowly approaching cars for a bit, then bend my whitening head and read another paragraph. Ormsby's book was published in time for the province's centenary in 1858. Well, the province has had a number of centenaries. Some people, unaware of the difference between a noun and an adjective, call them centennials. These are no doubt the same people who thought that the new millennium would start in January 2000. I wonder why they didn't just call it the new millennial?

Anyway, it was not the first time I had read Ormsby's book, but it seemed to me that it would make good reading while I waited for someone to come along and buy an hour of my mind. I had a lot to learn about that. I was already well into Chapter 7, "Jewel in Queen Victoria's Diadem," before anyone stopped, and it was already past nine at night.

I had watched what the girls did. When the car came to a stop at the curb in front of me, I went over and bent down, first looking to check for possible violence, then at the open side window, for negotiation. A thirtyish guy with a balding forehead leaned over and asked me what the hell I was doing.

"I been driving by here ten times today, and you're always there," he said.

"Just about," I said, ready to add words about a late lunch and several pees.

"What the hell are you doing?"

"I'm—"

"What's with the book? Always the book."

"I guess two things. How can a person stand around all day without a book to read—"

"Do it all the—"

"And it's kind of what you might call public information. I mean I wouldn't want people to get the wrong idea," I said.

There was a cop car approaching, slowly. It crossed my mind that this guy I was talking to was also a cop, hoping to entrap me. Thank goodness, I thought, neither of us had mentioned anything about money. The cop on my side of their car looked me up and down. He did not smirk, just kept that blank look the cops favour. The cop car pulled away, changing lanes without signalling.

"What wrong idea?" asked my guy in the car.

"Ah, well, I mean, I wouldn't want anyone to think I was just some low-IQ person blessed with a desirable body."

"Har har," he said. It looked as if he were preparing to drive away.

But he was my first possible sale. I decided to turn on my special gift for patter, the talent that had kept me in the classroom for two decades without disaster.

"Har har indeed," I said.

"So what would be the right idea?"

"Well," I said and made the throat sound that is often conveyed with the printed word "harrumph," "the other attractive people you see standing on corners up and down this street are seeking to sell, or rather rent, their bodies. I seek to sell or rent my mind."

"Hardy har har," he said and drove away.

"Conrad car car," I said into the night, regretting that no one within earshot would recognize the instant and multi-levelled wordplay.

When I was an undergraduate, the English professors let it be known that while they had to teach Hardy and Conrad in the same course, they reserved most of their respect for Conrad. He anticipated the psychological insights that would animate the major novelists and poets and filmmakers in the modern era, while Hardy was a typical Victorian with a ham-handed approach to characterization.

Secretly I had always preferred Hardy. He let you know how sad he was about the world. Conrad was interested in exhibiting moral conflicts, but you never got the sense that he cared all that much when his characters failed the test. Hardy, though blessed with an arch sarcasm, would often turn the screws of fate so hard on his people that you wanted to lament the lack of justice in the mortal world.

I thought about Hardy and Conrad for hours rather than reading in the evening light that made its way through the three layers of cloud over Vancouver. I did not get another prospective client, though several cars slowed as they passed my corner. I tried to look intellectually seductive, which consisted mainly of fiddling with my old brier and looking over the top of my glasses.

When I quit teaching, the university gave me the equivalent of two years' salary, which I banked and paid income tax on. I'm still pretty comfortable, though it will be over a decade till my pension kicks in. It was not out of financial desperation that I first stood on my corner. I suppose I might have needed something to fill my days now that I was no longer pretending to write my book on Matthew Arnold. But the main reason for my being there was a kind of curiosity. I wanted to know whether men who drove slowly down certain streets in downtown Vancouver were as lonely for knowledge as they were for physical spasms.

Maybe some of those people driving by in their slow, quiet cars were just too bashful or too little experienced to stop and bargain for knowledge. Maybe they had been enucleated by the popular culture, as people these days were calling it. I am one of the few old codgers who would insist that by "culture" they mean such things as literature, serious music, and the Quatroccento.

Danielle stopped to say hello on her way back from her coffee break at a shop next to the library. She was gorgeous in patent leather boots that zipped up to her thighs. She had a form-fitting jacket that seemed to be made principally of red egret feathers.

"Aubrey, how long are you going to carry out this feckless experiment?" she asked. "Why don't you go home, have a nice chocolate Ovaltine, and snuggle up with *The Decline and Fall of the Roman Empire?*"

"I've read it four times. I know it off by heart."

"Aubrey, you're going to give Richards Street a bad name," she said.

"Did you ever consider that I am hanging out here so that I can gaze at you just a block away?"

"I charge two hundred dollars an hour for gazing, chum."

She gave me her nicest smile, professional as it was, and patted my tweed shoulder with her long fingers, then headed toward her corner with a stride that would make a prelate pee his trousers.

The next night I was standing there with a cardboard coffee warming one hand, and a leather-bound copy of *Maud* in the other, when the same fellow stopped his car in front of me. The passenger-side window lowered without a sound, and he leaned over as best he could with his seat belt on.

"How much?" he asked.

Of course I had thought about this and had even come to a decision, but at that moment I could not remember what decision I had come to.

"Negotiable," I said.

"So, negotiate," he said.

"Hundred dollars."

"Fifty."

"Okay." I had been standing on that corner for two weeks without a sale.

"Get in."

I was as awkward as always, what with my briefcase and *Maud* and coffee. Over the past two weeks, and during my research the week before that, I had seen tall young women on high spiky shoes slip into the passenger seats of sedans and Jeeps and convertibles with a flourish of long naked legs and rippling hair. I banged my knee, dropped my coffee to the curb, and took three tries at closing the door. I didn't even try to do up the seat belt.

"Are we going to your place or a dark parking lot?" the guy asked.

"What? I mean where?" Things were still falling off my lap, etcetera.

"Usually we go to their place or a dark parking lot," he said. "Some of them don't want anyone going to their place. I never go to my place."

"Oh, I never go to my place on a first date," I said.

Which didn't make a lot of sense, because if I was going to sell my mind for fifty dollars the least I could do was let my reference books do half the work.

He pulled the car, and now I saw that it was a sport utility vehicle, into a lot down by the north side of False Creek.

"What sports do you find your vehicle useful for?"

"I don't know what you're talking about," he said, and he turned off the key. The lights went out and a glimmer was noticeable on the water. On the south side of False Creek young marrieds put their white plastic bags of fresh farm vegetables on the floor and began to consume three-dollar cups of coffee.

"I don't do any sports," said the guy. He was ducking his head under his retracting seat belt.

"Well, you have a sport utility vehicle," I said.

"I don't know what you're talking about," he said. "This don't seem much like fifty dollars' worth of mind to me."

I seized the opportunity to appear on top of the moment.

"The transaction starts when you hand me fifty dollars," I said.

He was a little overweight, and probably short, and shifted and heaved in the bucket seat as he reached into a side pants pocket for his thick wallet. He gave me two twenties, a five, three loonies, and some silver.

"That's what I've got," he said.

"I'll go fifty-five minutes," I said. I was wondering every second, What happens next? What do I do? I remembered certain experiences in the classroom.

"Okay, start," he said, and he might as well have looked at his wristwatch.

"You interested in the Austro-French Piedmontese War?" I asked, and a voice inside me asked why the hell I would come up with that.

He eyeballed me, then looked ahead at the shimmer on the black water. He shuffled his body behind the driver's wheel and put the palm of his right hand on his right thigh. Was he getting ready to put it on my left thigh? What the hell is the protocol? I asked myself.

I shuffled my body in the passenger seat.

"Well, it seems that an Italian patriot named Felice Orsini tried to assassinate the Habsburg emperor Franz-Josef. People were always trying to assassinate the Habsburg emperor. But when Napoléon III of France found out about it, he remembered that in his youth he too had fought for Italian independence. The Napoléons were always crying for liberty and such, while pulling off coups d'état, and here was a chance for Louis-Napoléon to get in good with the senators he had recently dumped. So in a secret meeting at Plombières, in July 1858, he pledged support for the Italian forces in the effort to free Lombardy and Venetia from the Austrian yoke. There are two villages called Plombières, in fact. There is Plombières-les-Bains, a dicky little place somewhat south of Nancy, and Plombières-lès-Dijon, just west of Dijon. Anyway, the Italians also had England on their side and could probably count on the Russians, who were pissed off with the Austrians for not being grateful enough for their help in an earlier scrap. Well, the Austrians blew this one. They should have just let well enough alone, but the emperor sent tough messages to Sardinia and Piedmont and ordered the Italians to forget it. This gave Napoléon III and Cavour all the excuse they needed to start the Austro-French-Piedmontese war. Well, both sides fought with stupidity and gallantry, and thousands of nicely dressed soldiers were killed, but eventually Napoléon beat Franz-Josef, and a little more of the Italian peninsula was removed from Austrian ownership. Then, of course, the Austrians had to worry about war with Prussia concerning territory in Denmark."

"Fascinating but confusing," said my client, still looking at the shimmer. The fingers of his right hand were tapping on his right knee.

"Interested in how the rumours of liberty in the north of Italy seemed to threaten the hegemony of the Pope?"

"I would find it fascinating."

"The Pope's people in Paris were concerned that—"

"I would find it fascinating, but I have to bring up a question that is bothering me," said my client with forty-some-odd minutes still on the clock.

The thought went through my mind that if I had had students more like him I might have still been in the classroom. Imagine: a student that brings up a question. Of course I smiled now and shuffled in my seat so that I was nearly facing him.

"Bring up your question, Mr.—"

"We don't do names in this kind of situation," he said.

"Of course not," I said. "What is your question?"

Unconsciously, probably, he now had his hands on the steering wheel. He did not, at first, look like the kind of man who spends a lot of time in reflective thought, but perhaps the species accommodates to the individual—a look of systematic consideration fitted itself to his very high forehead, and he spoke, still looking straight ahead through the windshield into patterns of exterior artificial light.

"You claim to be selling your mind," he said.

"Correct."

"You're a mind whore."

"If you have to put it in those terms."

He took a quick look at me and then looked back at his shimmer. Then back at me briefly.

"It seems to me," he said, "that with this Napoléon war in Italy, you are reciting a chain of events, a chain of events with a kind of cause and effect process, implied cause and effect, wouldn't you say?"

"Well, teaching is more than—"

"Teaching?"

"I mean."

"Here's what I'm thinking," he said. "All that stuff about alliances and battles and emperors, you could store it in your brain. Store it in your brain, and then bring some out whenever you need it."

"Ah, but it entails more than that. There's analytical thought and—"

"Bring it out whenever you want," he said.

"Sometimes it's easier than other times," I said.

His fingers were tapping fast on his thigh, both hands, both thighs. I was beginning to remember the stories I had heard from Danielle about bad tricks. No, that was an exaggeration, I decided. My client was still looking straight ahead, out the windshield, at the gleam. That did not make me comfortable, though.

"So what I'm saying is that's brain, that's not mind."

"Tell us what you mean by the distinction," I suggested.

"Us? Us? This isn't a classroom, professor; this is a date," said my client. I was really wishing that I knew his name, so that I could say his name at the beginning of each sentence from now on.

"Me," I said.

His fingers calmed down. Now he was running the palms of his hands up and down the dark cloth on his thighs. I reached inside my sweater and retrieved a roll of coughdrops from my shirt pocket. I extended it toward him and he looked and shook his head. So I popped two into my mouth.

I looked surreptitiously at my watch. Half an hour.

"The distinction," he said at last. "The distinction is this. Your brain is a network of gooey meat inside your head, very physical. But you do a million calculations, memory storing, arithmetic, sexual fantasies, and so on with your brain. And it's your brain. It's a personal thing, an individual thing, private. You follow me?"

I nodded, sort of forcing him to look over at me for a second.

"I got a brain. You got a brain. All God's children got brains. One each. Some better than others. When you die, that's it. That brain is toast."

"So to speak," I offered.

"Whereas the mind—that is (a) not personal and (b) not physical."

He sounded a little smug. Maybe a little apprehensive regarding how well he was doing, but also a little smug. Professors are used to getting that combination from people who want to argue with them.

"Proceed," I said. I had heard about johns who pay prostitutes a lot of money just so they can have someone to talk to.
But this was a little complicated, this date. I mean it was I who
was supposed to be talking for money.

He proceeded.

"Well, the way I look at it, the mind is something that
just—exists—out there, and we tap into it. With our brains,
I guess."

"I think I see where you're going," I said.

"Each of us can tap into various minds."

"Uh huh?"

"You've heard about them. The seventeenth-century mind.
The female mind. The northern European mind. Etcetera,
etcetera."

"The Habsburg mind and the Piedmontese mind," I
suggested.

"Ha ha. So what does it mean when you 'change your
mind'? I guess it's like changing your address or changing
your pants. You move out of one and into another. That's mind.
So that's why you can't really say that you're selling your
mind on the street, eh?"

"Well," I said in my defence, "I can't very well say I've got
brain for sale, can I?"

"Climb the stairs, try my wares."

"What?" I didn't know what he was saying.

Now his fingers were tapping like crazy.

"I figure you ought to give me back half my money," he said.

"Why?"

"Well, I figure brain is worth a lot less than mind, it being just (a) physical and (b) personal."

"Ah," I countered, making the "ah" last as long as possible while I thought about my next move. "Ah, but mind, well, you can just tap into mind like the internet. But brain is individual. If you get someone to deliver brain, that's a service. The provider has to make a living, eh?"

He was looking at me now instead of his old shimmer.

"Okay, I guess you're right," he said.

I smiled.

"How about a kiss?" he said.

What the hell. I gave him a kiss.

How Delsing Met Frances
and Started to Write
a Novel

As you know, Delsing was a poet before death, or so he persuaded himself and a few others, but once he tried to write a novel about his traditional US coming of age, all that sobbing tormented youth palaver, at least he thought about writing the novel, sitting around drinking beer with Bob Small in Vancouver 1960 or thereabouts and beginning in 1947, knowing, he said later, that he wasn't a US kid at all but only an early captive of their radio stations on the west coast. He decided that he had to do something of the sort to make use of his diary from those earlier years, though others, myself included, if you can guess who I am, suspected that he didn't have a diary that early but rather made the whole thing up, that included—as who doesn't, my friend? It all began with fancy quotations from Wordsworth, fixing him forever as a literary grandson, all that imbroglio those young writer chappies surround themselves with and some story about how it all *began* the first day of school, have mercy. Yep, the initiation, he steps into the new school building the first day where the halls are of course filled with kids yelling back and forth, all those *characters* you have to fill it up with, describing their shining shoes, new shirts and dresses, teeth flashing white from their suntanned faces. Grade seven, ah, high school, visions coming up on page 246 of sad high-school dances and soaking handkerchiefs in back of someone's drooping willow tree. . . .

They're all jostling around the drinking fountain—I don't know what names he gave them, but naturally he had it all worked out. Hey, you passed, eh, brown nose? Whaddya mean? They couldn't stand me down there in bygone elementary school anymore. Hell, he passed all right, old suck-up Delsing. Aw, shiut up, yeah, shiutup. Yer in high school now. Yet look at the sign, do not spit in the drinking fountain. They all spit in the drinking fountain, some dark red gum, too. But Delsing really was a sentimental boy, I mean the kid in school and the college kid essaying a book about it all, and so he tells us how he was sitting there mooning over "the old skinny caretaker" mowing the lawn—Christ, now this is sounding like a book review. Maybe you'll guess who this is after all—the grass is wet and the old guy can move the mower a few feet at a time before he has to bend over and thumb wet cuttings off the insides of the wheels. Naturally, Delsing the kid or that one later wants to tell the geezer to leave it till the grass gets dry. Really. You can see why he gets the way he gets later on, Ol' Delsing, as he'd call himself, the zooming aviator bypassing the kill because the chick's heart has its guns all jammed up. You know. At the same time he's listening to the teacher promising heavy homework, the old scare job he learns later himself in his own imitation of himself as a teacher. Gym shorts and sneakers. Woodwork and the tuba. Fifty cents for locker rental.

I think Delsing is already writing a novel at the time, about a kid who rises to the heights as a ballplayer and then throws it all away for some moral gesture involving a girl with bad posture. So he's already noting the rhythms of the talk around him. How do you like the dames in the class? (1947, dig?) Jesus, how come all the ugly dames are always in our class? Jeesus, did you notice the one in the Girl Guide suit? Agghh! Jesus, Scotch. Scotch or English or something. Scotch, I bet. God, did you hear her when he called the roll? Heah, sah. I never saw anything so funny. Jeesus, round glasses. Big thick brown stockings. Bet they come right up to her bush. Ah, she hasn't got a bush, she's Scotch. Jesus, PIGtails, pigtails, agghh again. Hey, Georgie, you sat right behind her. How could you stop laughing? He was studying already. Goddamn it, Red, you want to come outside and call me that? He was studying the dame with the PIGtails, that's what. We *are* outside, Delsing. What's her name, Delsing? How the fuck should I know? Hey, you said fuck.

Trying to be one of the gang, you see, though he has his private conscience against it.

Frances, her name's Frances. The Freak. Yep, Frances the Freak with pigTAILS. Let's have a Coke before we buy them books.

So the story has to go, he arrives at home, with all the homey realistic touches such as a screen door. He pushes the door open awkwardly because his arms are filled with books and erasers, which he dumps on the table after which he instantaneously snaps on the square black shortwave radio. This conversation or something like it ensues, because we're supposed to get a gradual introduction to Delsing's other interests and family:

That you, George?

What happened to the Red Sox?

Oh for heaven sake, come into the kitchen.

(Where I am, my dear, picturesquely and characteristically standing at the sink, peeling apples to fill five empty pie shells on the sinkboard. Aw, Mum, yer just like my mum, back then in 1947, when the *Saturday Evening Post* had covers you wouldn't be ashamed to pin on the back porch wall—)

What occurred to the Red Sox?

I don't know; the Yankees beat somebody.

Philadelphia. (I mean, we didn't even know where these places were, really. Chicago was somewhere in the east, where people hopelessly referred to it as the capital of the Middle West.) You didn't hear the Red Sox score?

I heard it but I can't remember.

Jeeze.

What?

I guess St. Louis beat the Dodgers again, eh?

I wouldn't know. Will you take your things into your room and then come back and set the table for supper?

Yeah. Hey, did you fill the woodbox again? Jeeze, I was just going to do that as soon as I got home.

Well, I've just about given up on that score. I asked you to get it done before you went to school.

Jeeze, well—

Just hurry up and set the table. How much did your school supplies cost?

Eleven something. I gotta have five bucks for books and fifty cents for locker fees, and I gotta have a new pair of running shoes.

What's wrong with the ones you've been using all summer?

(You see? Mothers—)

Ah, Mum, you can't take gym with low sneakers. I gotta have a pair of basketball shoes.

I think you can make do with your current ones. I can't be buying you a pair of running shoes every few months. Now set the table, or do I have to do that, too?

Ah (and under his breath a swear word we don't have to remember)—

(Though in his novel he filled it all in with extra lines of dialogue and little bits about how the young fellow felt, the embarrassment as tears squeezed below his eyelids, etc. Don't forget, he was reading all those 1935 American novelists with their fat books.)

As a matter of fact, Bob Small copied this out and sent it over to me. It's an actual fragment from somewhere in the beginning of this great lost manuscript. Small used to come and stand over Delsing and watch the fingers flying, two of them, he reported, every night after college in a basement on Fourteenth Avenue. This is it, *ver,* as they say, *batim. . . .* Oh the guys kidded about her the first day of school and I didn't say anything because I wasn't too sure about my position in the gang, I got good marks and they all thought I studied too much, which was really funny, thinking about how my mother used to be after my ass for not studying at all—"I wish you would work up to your ability so you could really make me proud of you, there'll come a time later on when you'll wish you'd worked harder"—and of course I found that to be a true prophecy, but I'd try to study and pretty soon I'd be reading the sports page over again and pretty soon I'd be playing my little ragged dice baseball game, keeping all the scores and American and National League standings, Cincinnati and the Browns in the World Serious that year, and then it would be time to get the "Game of the Day" re-created on Armed Forces Radio on the shortwave, and later reading Zane Grey and Thorne Smith under the covers with a flashlight

(Shit, we all did that, Delsing)

and trying to name all the forty-eight states, and trying to think of baseball players whose names started with all the letters of the alphabet—Abrams, Berra, Cox, DiMaggio (Dom), Evers—usually I fell asleep halfway

through at Musial or Newsome. I guess the guys didn't
notice I never got into the kidding about her at all. They all
thought I was kind of stupid in the sense of weird, anyway—
I wouldn't smoke cigarettes or steal comic books at the
Rexall, I wouldn't even be the bad guy when we were playing
guns, because I was going to be a noble crimefighter chasing
down crooks running along shadowed alleys carrying sacks
with $ signs on them.

It wasn't that I had a you might say positive feeling for her.
Knowing me now, you'd know I didn't like anyone, or I didn't
extend my favours to anyone, except Roberto Small (he of
earlier acquaintance, you'll remember, Ol' Bob as I used to call
him in the cute days, hard to believe he later became a drinking
buddy and now owns a house in the East End of Vancouver)—
he was second in command at one time of an organization
called the Coyotes, still my favourite animal—

(Delsing says
Coyote still is, in the hip animist respectful Indian religion
way, in all likelihood)

—though he could never learn to use a
sword and shield, essential heroic devices carved from wood,
but he was more than fair with a bow and arrow, causing my
seldom-encountered secret envy. It wasn't that I liked her,
Frances the Freak, but I just wouldn't enter into the shithouse
talk about her—there'd been something wrong with me ever
since I'd turned four years old and received the intimation that
I might bear the responsibility of being the second coming
of Christ, really.

But I noticed she'd been picked out by the gods to be related somehow to the old caretaker who was out trying to mow the wet lawn the first day of school (accept my prayers, old bugger)—I wished I could remove the round glasses from her head and throw them into the teacher's green wastebasket, give her a pair of Canadian girl socks (aw, them white bobby sox, how I love the pink or brown bare swell of calf above them even now!), unbraid her hair, and instruct her on the way to say here, sir. (Never to me, you'll understand, I was so pure, Jesus at age eleven going on twelve.) She sat in front of me, a brown little girl, though two inches taller than I was, wouldn't look up from her scarred desktop except when her name was called, sitting with her hands in her neutral lap as if they were both broken at the wrists lying there like Plasticene blobs, her legs tucked under her desk, ankles crossed. Her legs were straight, and they didn't taper down to the ankles the way grade seven calls for. I didn't know why I should be interested in her (though all or most of the ladies since then looked a little odd somewhere)—I *wasn't* interested in her as a girl, if that's what she was, or the English equivalent of same, aw, sad sentence, hung around corners of my own deceitfulness, except that she was so goddamned helpless. At home she would in all likelihood sit beside her mother all day in the kitchen and never say a word save amen at grace.

That first day I didn't even get a look at her hung-down face except when she stood up after class was dismissed to go get supplies from the Rexall downtown, and then she still had it hanging down, braids in front of her shoulders, so I didn't see much other than those Raggedy Ann glasses. In fact there wasn't much to her face, it wasn't very bright, it even looked dirty, though in fact it wasn't, but there was a smear of light freckles over her nose and under the rims of her glasses on her flat cheeks. She looked sad like Shirley Temple, but not chubby like Shirley Temple, more like a droopy Welsh setter dog such as the one that used to mope and limp around behind Small before it got blind in both eyes and started to slobber all over you and finally had a fit and perished one day like a dirty sweatshirt flat and skinny under an apricot tree in the neighbour's orchard.

The stupidest thing, you'll have noticed, was that Christly Girl Guide uniform—they all looked like old thrown-away machine-shop smocks that some crone got and sewed patches onto. This one was too loose, the shirt hung crooked, and it was baggy all over the front. I didn't know why they made them wear these hideous things (brown or navy blue!) to school all day when Guides wasn't till seven at night, though she had an excuse because she lived three miles south of town on Highway 97, and later I found out too that she had to go over to her granny's house and have supper, feeding her granny's blind old cocker spaniel all the way through the meal (Lawrence was a town full of blind dogs and pool-playing Indian guys with French names). So I felt sorry for her

(aw, that's how you always started on these things, Delsing, you can't have an emotional moment unless you can find a poor object of your Mercy) because she had to wear such a thing, but she probably didn't know enough to feel sorry for herself, any more than her celestial uncle the old caretaker bent on his arthritic breakable legs to thumb wet grass cuttings off the twisted blades of the mower.

I followed her out of the room and watched her walk all by herself (later she would solve that problem by becoming an office-holder in every club in school and later college, Miss Responsible) after a big mob of girls who were of course squealing and giggling even before they got out into the hall. When I joined the guys at the drinking fountain full of tooth-marked gum, I forgot all about her till they started in on the Freak business. To my unwelcome shame, I kept my quiet, remembering that Jesus rode not a foaming stallion but a droop-headed donkey.

(Yeah, Dels, and the trouble with you is you never rode droop-headed Frances, as Rouge said in his poem years later before he died.)

After supper that night my mother, Lorna, asked me whether I'd met anyone new in class—what kind of question is that for a mother?—and I mentioned the girl from Jolly England and what the lads in the corridors called her. She asked me whether I called her that too, and I was mad or shy or something and said sure I did, so she bawled me out as usual, and complained about me to my radio and newspaper dad.

Old Bottles

When people started raising a fuss about the place being built by Mr. Weatherall, they should have been taking a good look at themselves and the town they were living in. All in all, it was pretty silly, what he was doing, but the complainers were living in Hummer by choice, most of them, and that wasn't exactly the most rational choice in the world. Of course I lived here too, still do. Nobody has ever accused me of having too many smarts.

If you haven't been to Hummer, British Columbia, you haven't been nowhere, as they say. In fact there is some joker who keeps putting up signs reading NOWHERE on the highway at both ends of town, and the village commissioners keep yanking them down. They must have a good pile of them by now. It's kind of normal, and I think most people here like it. So I'd like to impress you with the fact that Mr. Weatherall was not the only loony in town. And Myrna Weatherall was not the only victim of looniness.

In fact, whoever started Hummer probably left the legacy for all the bush-heads who have cropped up since. Hummer is in the middle of the great semi-arid region of the BC Interior. They never stop telling you that, in school and in all the Chamber of Commerce propaganda. In fact, we're officially at the northern tip of the Great Sonoran Desert. You could check it out in the *National Geographic*. So maybe we were meant to be Mexicans, maybe that's our problem, we are in the wrong place.

Because for a place that is supposed to be in a desert, we sure get a lot of rain. Not rain the way you probably understand rain, but a kind of heavy mist that hangs around and takes its time falling, kind of like our government in Victoria, but it comes down eventually, so all summer long your lawn is too wet to sit on, and it takes all day to mow it.

The problem is that Hummer sits at the bottom of a huge rock bluff about half a mile high. In the old days there was a mine at the base of the cliff, and after a while there was a company store, and pretty soon a couple of bars. This was before we got truly Canadianized. And then a nice two-storey farmhouse where quite a few ladies from California took up residence. Why some bright soul didn't decide to locate his place of business a mile up the valley, I don't know. He probably figured the miners would be flat broke before they made that mile, I suppose.

Anyway, what's at the bottom of Hummer bluff is only half the problem. The other half is what's at the top. There's a creek up there, a big creek. Some people call it a river, and some people call it a lot worse names than that. I'd love to tell you what my husband called it, but I don't dare. It was really funny, but it isn't the sort of thing a school principal's widow is supposed to say. Maybe where you live, but not in the great semi-arid region of BC.

Of course when the creek, let's call it, gets to the edge of the bluff, it turns into a waterfall. A very pretty one, too, for the first thousand feet, or I guess you say the first such-and-such metres now. But then it just disappears. Disappears as a waterfall, I mean. It hits an enormous jumble of scraggly rocks and promptly takes off into the air. That's how we get our famous mist. The sun shines just about every day in this part of the country, and the few visitors tell us it's really beautiful here, with a trillion little reflecting beads of water above us and the never-ending rainbow. And in the summer people from Kamloops or Ashcroft say my oh my aren't you lucky, it's so cool here, why back home it was a hundred in the shade all last week.

In the winter the creek just about disappears. The top of the bluff is covered with giant green icicles, and we get snow from time to time. But as soon as the spring melt starts up in the Sawtooth Mountains, we start praying for our hairdos. They sell a lot of hairspray in little towns in the Interior, but nowhere as much as they sell in Nowhere. I don't mean all this to suggest that Mr. Weatherall was only a kind of product of this crazy geography. I just can't help running on sometimes, espe-cially on days like this in the early summer.

The Weatheralls lived right across the street from us, so people would try to enlist our help in organizing some kind of protest. But there is more griping and head shaking than organized protesting in small towns, at least there was in those days. Beside which, I wasn't all that angry about his bottles. A little nirked, somewhat amused, but not angry, not really.

He started with the front fence. When we came to this house the Glendennies lived over there, and they had a hedge made of lilacs across the front, purple and white. They smelled wonderful in the spring evenings when there was more moonlight than moisture in the air. But about two years after buying the place, old Mr. Weatherall, in his very old business suit complete with vest, started cutting them down and rooting them up. I thought maybe he was going to put in boxwood, or maybe Myrna Weatherall was allergic to strong-smelling flowers. But about a month later the first bottles appeared.

They were green wine bottles, and he was making a fence out of them, laying them on their sides with the bottoms outward, toward us. I don't know where he was getting all the wine bottles. I never thought people in Hummer were all that keen on wine. More the beer and rye whisky sort, I would have thought. If the Weatheralls drank all that wine themselves, they would have been dead long before he got the fence up to his knees, and it was four and a half feet high when it was done the first time. As a matter of fact, I knew a few people, the only wine fanciers I knew, and they would always be pestering everyone they knew to save their bottles because they made their own wine. I used to save my Christmas bottle for Louise Perks, but Louise is someone I'll have to save for another story, if I ever finish this one.

Now every few weeks I would see Mr. Weatherall, huffing and puffing, or so I assumed, his belly sticking out so you could see some white shirt below his vest, carrying a couple of shopping bags up the hill from Main Street, and even more rarely I would see him laying his new empties on the fence. A few times I saw Myrna Weatherall looking at him from between the drapes of her front room, just as I was.

I guess it was a little over a year later that the front fence was finished. At least so it would seem, because he had by then started on the back fence. The back of their yard faced onto the playground of the old school that had been converted into a community hall. He was doing the back fence with brown wine bottles. He must have been saving them in his garage or basement. But he had to abandon the brown for a while because someone had attacked his green one.

Some people thought it was the work of a real-estate vigilante group, but I figured it was stone-throwing kids or some of those young louts who bomb around small towns in noisy cars. Nowadays you see these cretins in American cars with fat back tires and the rear end jacked up high. In those days they had the rear end trailing as low as their own IQs. They usually drive around impressing each other and pretending they're looking for girls, but really they're looking for something to break, usually something that belongs to the school or to old people. I figured they probably took a tire iron or their own foreheads to Mr. Weatherall's fence.

But even if his fence was made of glass, Mr. Weatherall wasn't. A few months later he had replaced all the broken bottles, and a month after that he had made a heavy wire frame around the whole fence. This is when I started to react a little against the idea. I had never really minded the bottles, because I'm not one of those people who can't stand change. When the Portuguese refugees moved in and started painting their houses pink and aqua, I sort of enjoyed it, especially when it brought out the worst of people in letters to the *Bulletin*. Heaven knows, people probably wondered how I put up with my husband's scarecrow in our back garden. He dressed it up in my old wartime girdle and other unmentionables. He said that would scare anything with wings, fins, or feet. Never bothered me at all. But maybe I should save my husband for another time.

No, the bottles hadn't bothered me, but the wire around them did. I don't know whether this was because it was inherently tacky or because it showed something about the kind of town I was living in. At least I didn't have to look very often at the wire around his back fence. Not until he cut the trees down.

For some reason a lot of the towns in the semi-arid region of the Interior are full of Siberian elms. I don't think they are native to the area. Most of them act as shade trees around the edge of people's yards, and in Hummer, one supposes, they also act as a kind of umbrella. They grow prodigiously, so people are busy pruning them severely every February. Mr. Weatherall was a pruner until the third year of what I came to refer to as his project. That spring he cut his elms right down to ground-level stumps. His purpose might have been to give the filtered sunlight a chance to shine through his bottles. Or he might have had in mind making his handiwork easier to see. If that's what he had in mind, it certainly worked. The letters to the editor were now full of bottles and trees.

With the trees gone, we could now see the renovation of his garage. He spent his fourth summer replacing three of its walls with beer bottles. You'll remember that in those days we had the tall bottles with the long necks, and they were brown and green and sometimes clear. He was becoming more daring in his design now, making borders and accents in green, and a big white *W* on the wall facing the community hall. I had not seen Myrna Weatherall's face at the window for a year.

As you can imagine, the weather has never been a big topic of conversation in Hummer, but Mr. Weatherall's project certainly was in those days. A lot of it would go like this:

"There should be some kind of law. People don't want to live next to a freak show."

"We moved up here because Mickey Chadwick filled up his yard with old tires and crank cases. And now I have to live three doors down from an old idiot and his bottles."

"Well," said my husband, "a fellow needs something to do when he's retired."

When my husband offered one of his sentences in a conversation, there was often a general silence for about the time it takes to count to ten. Then someone would edge back toward where they were before.

"I just feel sorry for Myrna Weatherall most of all," said Louise.

Not that anyone ever went calling on Mrs. Weatherall, me included. I felt as if I wanted to, in a way, living right across the street and all. But I never went over there after they bought the place off the Glendennies, and now I felt as if it would be a little obvious. She would know it was either because I was worried about my neighbourhood or about her. At least I would feel as if she would be thinking that way.

What with all the conversation going on, and the letters in the *Bulletin* that never named names but referred to certain "community values," it got to be that we all learned a little history, or at least rumours, about the Weatheralls. The most persistent story was that Mr. Weatherall used to own an orchard down in Lawrence, and as the orchard became less and less productive, his house turned from wood into glass. When he lost the orchard he lost the house too, and when the new owner took over, he bull-dozed the whole project and half the trees and went into onions.

"Maybe the village commissioners should advertise the bottle house as a tourist attraction," said someone.

"When was the last time you saw a tourist in Hummer?" asked someone else. And it was true; Hummer was not a resort town by a long shot. People went to Windermere for the hot springs and Penticton for the beaches, but nobody was going to come to Nowhere for the mist *or* the bottles.

By the end of the fifth summer he had transformed the front of the house. The porch and the front wall were now sparkling clear bottles that once held gin and vodka. Mrs. Weatherall's abandoned window was gone. You had the sense that you could see through the wall, but you really couldn't. You also had the sense that there were a lot of strong spirits passing through people's bodies around here.

I had to admit to myself that I was starting to get annoyed, though I was still interested. How was he going to do the roof? I wondered. What would he replace the lawn with? But I was not happy when the trees came down. What he was doing was in no way pretty. Later, when the commissioners did try to make something of it, the term "folk artist" came up, but that sort of idea won't last long in a town like this, and it wasn't true anyway. I mean, Mr. Weatherall might have been within his rights. He might have been very dedicated to his project. But he was an old loony. I think every town in the Interior has its share of very visible loonies.

I really began feeling negative when he started on his towers. Two towers in his front yard, one on each half of his lawn. And they weren't made of glass bottles. They were made of those light plastic bottle-shaped containers you get liquid detergent and bleach in. All different colours, bright, unnatural colours, and short words all over them. I suppose the young nit who was talking about folk art (he was a teacher here in the junior high school for two or three years), I suppose he considered Mr. Weatherall some kind of poet now.

Louise and my other friends no longer carped about community values when they came to our house for bridge. Each one just looked at me with her head on an angle, reminding me that I had been a little slow in criticizing the reclamation project across the street.

"Four Lux," said Louise.

"What?" Three heads on angles.

"I mean four clubs," she said.

I put three spoons of sugar in her coffee.

The towers went up faster than any of the walls or fences had. They were soon a little over ten feet high and the brightest objects in the Hummer mist. At least he didn't have floodlights to show them up at night. Not yet.

If I had been Myrna Weatherall, this is when I would have taken off. But she didn't. Maybe she didn't have any relatives in the country. We never heard anything about their family, whether they had any kids or whatever. Maybe she was just the kind of woman who doesn't ever think of herself as a separate unit. There were plenty of them in the miners' families around here. There might be a few left even now.

Maybe if she had gone, her husband would have replaced her with a woman built out of Pepsi bottles.

I didn't have a much more human picture of her than that myself. They'd been living there for just about seven years, and I hadn't passed more than a hundred words with her. Of course she didn't play golf and she didn't play bridge. She didn't have any children in school and she didn't own a car. Once in a blue moon you would see her in the post office or the drugstore, and then you would exchange a bashful nod or hello. No one ever said anything about the weather, so you couldn't start a conversation that way.

I mean, what was I supposed to do, phone her up and compliment her on the towers? Yet I really wanted to talk to her now, find out whether she needed something, I suppose.

Find out whether all this bottle business was doing something, well, awful to her. To hell with it, I decided, I would forget my little fears and shames and go. So when my brother Fred brought us our annual supply of apples from his orchard in Summerland, I figured I would explain that I had too many; the extras wouldn't make it through the winter. Then why would I be offering them to her instead of my friends or the school? Well, what was I supposed to do? So I loaded a box on the neighbour kid's wagon that was always out in the alley and rolled on over to the bottle house.

I thought, well, this is going to be embarrassing anyway, so I might as well go the whole route. People in Hummer don't use front doors very often. A front door is for business, and a back door is for friends. Maybe I didn't want to get too close to those towers, either. I pulled the wagon to the end of the block and around to the community-hall yard, up to the Weatheralls' back door. The back steps were made of flat whisky bottles.

When I rapped on the frame of the absent door, it was not Myrna's but old Mr. Weatherall's face that appeared at the top of the basement stairs. I thought he would be embarrassed too, or at least surprised, but he simply smiled, wiped his fingers on his burdened vest, and gestured for me to enter.

"I've brought some apples," I said. He was still smiling, like someone who has something to sell or to show off. "My brother, bless his soul, brought us more than we can possibly. . . ." I put my head on an angle to indicate the wagon at the bottom of the steps.

I wanted to see everything in the house I hadn't been in for nine years, but the situation was so uncomfortable I couldn't really register anything. I don't know what I was expecting, but it did seem rather ordinary. Mrs. Weatherall's influence, I gathered.

"Apples, oh, yes. That is kind of you, Missus," said Mr. Weatherall in an English accent common to towns in the Interior.

"Mrs. Weatherall, is she here?" I really needed the familiar presence, the help of another woman to get me through this.

Mr. Weatherall went out and looked more closely at the apples, but he didn't bring them inside. My embarrassment was not being taken care of at all.

"If Mrs. Weatherall, if Myrna is out, I can come back later and get the wagon. That'll give me an excuse to talk to her," I said and made things worse with a foreshortened chuckle.

"She is here," he said.

"Oh, is she not well? If there is something I can get for her. . . ."

"No," he said. "She passed away."

I just stood there.

"She's been gone for a week."

I just stood there. She's here, he had said. She's gone, he said now.

"I'm sorry. I didn't hear anything about it." I hadn't seen her for months.

"She was ill for a long time," he said more conversationally. "For years, really."

"I'm awfully sorry. I should have come over long ago."

"Yes. Come," he said and indicated the front part of the house.

I just stood there.

"Come, please," he said.

I followed him to the ordinary English-immigrant living room and through it onto the front porch and down the glass steps to the front yard. The bottles of the fence pointed toward us. The towers glistened with dew in the bright filtered sunlight.

"She is here," he said, and now he turned to face me with his hands behind his back, with his weight on his toes. Like a curator.

The cement walk between the two halves of the lawn had been removed and replaced with sod that hadn't taken yet. Except at the halfway point, right between the two towers. There was a brown rectangle, three feet by six feet, rising about eight inches above the grass. Made of medicine bottles. Hundreds of them.

"Mr. Weatherall," I said.

He was not smiling now, just standing with his hands behind his back, surrounded by his work. I was not embarrassed anymore. The medicine bottles were utterly clean, utterly exact. It was perfectly symmetrical. It was beautiful.

"That's illegal," I said.

Of course you know roughly what happened after that. The village and the police and the lawyers and the undertakers all did their business. The town was scandalized better than ever. The *Bulletin* had to add another page for letters. The

Vancouver papers picked up the story, and for once we did have some tourists.

My friends decided it was my turn to host the bridge game for three weeks in a row. I never saw such bad bridge playing. Everyone kept looking across the street and talking about Myrna as if they had known her.

"He told you she was sick for years?" asked Louise.

"That's what he told me," I said.

"Do you think they moved here for their health?"

"Louise!" Some people are a lot less embarrassed after the fact.

"So all the time she was in that house sick, he was going all over God knows where, collecting bottles," she said.

"I think that in some crazy way," I said, pointedly slapping down the ten of diamonds, "he was building a memorial for her."

"Well," said Louise, looking with disappointment at my lead, "I for one wouldn't want a memorial made of Oxydol and Fab."

But I think I was right. Everyone, of course, wondered what would become of Mr. Weatherall. There was never any question of sending him to jail, the poor old loony. Some people expected him to move away to unknown parts. Others thought he would waste away or commit suicide, as often seems to happen in cases like that, though how many cases have you heard of like that?

But he didn't. He just stayed alone in that peculiar house. He never added another bottle, and he didn't replace the ones that were broken. Someone did remove the towers, or persuaded him to. I don't remember anyone making up for their neglect by going to visit him. Four years after his wife died, he joined her in the municipal cemetery. A week after he was gone, the kids and hot-rod goons went after the rest of his project. A year later the village took the place for taxes because no one was ever found as their heir. First they tried to sell the place, then they tried to make it a curio, then they bull-dozed it. My husband once made eyes at it, but I didn't know whether he was serious or teasing me. I stared him down, just to be safe. And I also became much more definite about that scarecrow of his. It seemed as if he spent the whole next summer waving his arms at the birds in the garden. I cherish that picture of him. And I miss him a lot.

At the Store

When she had been a small girl she had played in the snow, the way all the children her age played, happily, without a thought, young. It was the world they lived in nearly half the year, the snow. It came in the wind and stuck to the sides of the horses. It melted after a while on your eyelashes, and it covered dead things in smooth white hills. At nightfall it lost everything when it lost its whiteness, and it was replaced by cold.

Even cold was all right, because there were two more children in her tent, and a mother. There were dogs outside in the wind, and in the morning they were alive. In the morning it was still cold, but if you were a small girl you could hardly wait to go outside with nothing on your hair.

But now she was not a girl. She was a woman who thought about death while she did her work. She took the skins off animals and decided what to do with the things she had in her opposite hands. The ghost people at the store were interested in skins. The other things would be eaten by people and dogs.

But she was thinking about death. This death did not have an owner yet. It had a place to go, but she had made no decision, so it just waited. She could keep it herself, herselves in reality. If she ate the death herself, it would also feed the form inside her. Inside her it was dark, so the skin of that form had no colour. She did not know whether it was a ghost or a person. Was it going to be white like a ghost, or was it going to be brown like the people?

Or she could take the death with her and visit the ghost who might be its father. The ghosts and their store were the market for death. They brought it from some other earth and sold it in their stores, the ghosts. They took the skins from animals and gave the people death in return. The father of the form inside her was not as strong as a person, but he was stronger than she had been. He had told her something in his ugly language, and he had offered her the drink. Many drinks. Then when the real world slid away from her feet, he had shown her how strong death can be.

After that she had stayed away from her own man for a week and then another week. He was not a tender person but he was thoughtful. She could see him thinking, and sometimes she thought she would tell him about the ghost in the back room of their store. But the form arrived inside her before she made that decision. Now she carried her skinning knife with her all the time, but she had never been back to the store. She was thoughtful now, and she was thinking of the store. Probably the ghost would like to go into the back room with her again, but this time she would be carrying the knife she used to separate skin from animals.

And now she hated the cold. When she had been a girl she would walk in the snow with bare feet and nothing on her hair. Now she wrapped her feet and she always wore a cloth over her head.

The ghost had said some things in the people's language, but these words sounded ugly from his mouth.

You want this, he had said.

Make some noise, he had said. You can make some noise.

But she had made no sound. She did not want what he had for her, but the earth was gone from her feet. Afterward he had tried to fix her clothing, but he did not know how. She went home with her feet naked, but there had been no snow yet on the ground.

Now the snow was as high as a dog except for the footpaths, and she was wearing wrappings on her feet. And she was carrying her skin knife all the time. She walked halfway to the store and then she turned back. It could be for both of them, for both of them and the form inside her, the death.

What is this? You think that you can get away with this? If you think that you can tell this kind of story, a Native's story, if you think you can just up and use a Native person's experience and make a fiction of it, you are no better than the exploitive white traders you pretend to condemn. If you try to argue that you are not using the first person, you are probably wearing a forked tongue in your mouth.

That is just plain theft. You might as well be taking away really good valley land and using the indigenous women for your sport.

Do you not have any stories of your own to tell? Maybe you should forget fiction and just go into real estate. Become a developer. You seem to have the talent for it.

It was her second winter in this dreadful land. During the summer she had worn cloth over every inch of her body and a veil hanging in front of her face. The insects formed clouds in front of her as she walked along the footpaths that were constantly threatened by the deep forest on both sides. But the winters were worse. The snow and darkness and cold that murdered the insects would never be fed enough lives to keep them away from the crack under the casement.

From the forest came the sudden snap of a frozen tree. The dogs whimpered as they walked. There was blood between their claws.

She was the wife of a junior officer in Her Majesty's Royal Engineers. Her fate was to live in places devoid of civilization, and then to move on when the first road becomes passable. So it had been in Guiana. But in Guiana she had never seen a four-horse carriage slip over a lake turned to ice. She had never seen that shade of grey-blue before coming here.

And now she was thinking about shame and death. She was wondering whether what she was faced with was a choice. Would her death erase the shame or just make it longer remembered in her husband's detachment?

All the windows were covered with ferns of ice, except the window nearest the stone fireplace. There she stood and looked out at the bright light off the snow. Her eyes were not

really seeing, but they received the image of the company
store, the snowshoes hanging outside the thick door made of
vertical logs, the smoke rising straight as a flagpole from the
chimney.

She had not been back to that store since the horror. Her
pointed boots had not left a print that pointed toward that store.

What she could absolutely not understand or remember
was how that man persuaded her to drink the intoxicant.
Certainly it had fallen to her as an officer's wife to sip a glass
of sherry from time to time, and even a bit of rum in strong
fruit juices on summer evenings in Guiana. What was it she
had tasted in the front room and the back room of the store? It
was something made by the company itself, with the
company's name on the label. Whisky? Something strong. It
tasted terrible, but for some reason she had needed it. Probably
whisky.

Now she remembered, looking through a pane of glass with
crystals of ice in each of the four corners, now she remembered the heat. She had been wearing cloth on every inch of
her body, and a moment after entering that back room to look
at the newly arrived fabric, she fell through the heat and would
have struck her head on the plank floor had not something
caught her, a pile of rolled carpet perhaps, perhaps the bare
arms of that man. She woke with whisky, it must have been
whisky, falling down her chin, whisky in her throat. She
coughed, and he held her head, the hat made of mesh and
flowers having fallen somewhere, in the crook of his arm,
more whisky at her lips.

Here, you want this, he said.

She could not get to her feet. The long skirt tangled with her legs. She was leaning on his arm. She tried to speak, but there was whisky in her throat. She had tasted something like this before, years ago, when a young man in uniform looked at her with moonlight behind his eyelashes.

I have to get up. Help me, she said.

Here, you want a little more of this. He spilled some on the front of her dress, and now, looking out at smoke standing above a chimney, she thought he had done it on purpose. She was blushing now, or she felt the heat from the flames on her face as she stood in front of the window. She looked down and wondered whether she was beginning to show.

Make all the noise you want to, the man had said. I like noise, he said.

So it takes centuries for women to take possession of their own stories, to undo the centuries of male hegemonic proprietorship, and you have not heard the message? The day when men can claim authority in the rendering of women's history and consciousness is long over. What delusion are you suffering that makes you think that there can be anything authentic in your telling a story from an oppressed woman's point of view?

Why do you not just continue your own male tradition, give us tales of derring-do and boldness, valiant men on a quest, terrible trials by fire and sea monsters? Give us the usual battles and explosions and adventurers conquering the hostile land.

Maybe you should think this over, start the story again, but tell it from the point of view of the rapist in the stockroom. That's what the whole male literary project is about, is it not?

A year ago he could not have encountered a fresh deep snowfall without wanting to make his mark in it, to fall on his back and make an angel, or to roll big snowballs and construct a fort for protection against the scalp hunters in the forest, to stockpile snowballs hard as ice for defence against his schoolmates.

But this winter he hated the cold and the deep blue sky with crystals falling in the low sunlight. He walked on the trodden path rather than striding into the knee-deep snow. When there were errands to be done, he walked to them with his face forward and angled downward. A year ago he would have dallied. He would have stopped to throw a snowball at a jay on the slat fence behind the big stable.

His mother sent him on errands. It was her errand that took away his angel and his snow fort.

Now he did not know what he was. He thought he was no longer a young boy, but he knew that he had to be. He was none of the alternatives, not a man, grown, not a girl. He only had to touch himself to know that. He touched himself more often than he had done a year ago. This winter he touched himself often, and tried to handle the images that appeared. Were these images behind his forehead, the bone of his forehead, or were they out there, just a little measure before his forehead and his shut eyes?

He tried to handle the images, to bring back the clear picture of a year ago, the shameful image of his schoolteacher. She was ten years older than he, and now, although he went to school five days of every week and saw her from every side, her image fell away from him like earth falling away from a person's feet. Now as he warmed his winter hand against his private skin, the wrong image appeared. He insisted on the schoolteacher, but the wrong image appeared. He was among the rolled carpets in the back room of the company store again.

And he would remove his hand, put his hand behind him, even. But the image of that man in the back room of the store remained almost clear, even when he forced his eyes open wide, and his flesh did not ease.

When his mother sent him to the store he walked there with his face down, straight through the deeper snow if the trail took a turn. He walked there with his hands in his pockets. His mother threatened to sew his pockets closed, and she gave him a new pair of deer-hide mitts. He walked with his hands in his pockets, and left his mitts beside the kitchen door. He carried a knife on his belt, inside his coat.

On his way to the store he conjured an image of the man in the back room, and now he was killing that man with his knife, driving the knife hard through thick clothing, through thick flesh and bones, deep into his heart, right through the man's heart. But while he conjured this image, his flesh stirred again down there. Now he did not know, while he was walking toward the store, whether he made this image so that he could be killing his enemy or so that he could feel his flesh move. He was thirteen years old, after all. Even a year ago he had sat in his classroom and feared that he would be called upon to stand up and read to the class.

Now he did not know what he was, walking to the store.

But he was carrying his knife.

But when he got to the store, the man looked at him as if he did not recognize him. He looked at him as if he were only his mother's son come to fetch flour and dried apricots and tea leaves.

It was hard to raise his head. He placed the handwritten order on the counter and waited. He did not have to put money in the man's hand because there was a receipt book with his father's name hand-lettered on the spine. Sometimes he did raise his head, to watch the man while he gathered the things. He looked perfectly ordinary. He looked like a man who did ordinary things.

The tea leaves were kept next to the spirits with the company name on the bottles. Schoolboys are fascinated with strong spirits. They tell lies about the amounts they have drunk, and they steal it whenever they can. They are unlikely to demur when a man invites them to share a drink. Dares them to.

What do you think the chances are that a so-called straight writer, a breeder, a middle-class man living a sheltered life, will ever get a subject like this right? What do you know about marginalized sexual orientation? And more important, what gives you the right to pretend that you are privileged to eavesdrop on the psyche of a boy in such a situation?

Are there not enough stories for you to tell in the so-called normal majority society? Are you so much driven by the desire to keep up on fashionable subject matter that you will burgle the lives of thousands of young men that are bullied out of everything a lifetime should offer them?

You would be well advised to keep to your own side of the fence you people built. Go and make lots of babies, and leave the writing to us. Maybe some of those babies will join us.

He walked around and around in the new snow. He made giant steps. He walked backward. He made a big circle and then he made a radius and another radius and another until he had a pie. There were no other boys there to play the pie game, but a game was not his reason for walking around in the new snow. He was trying not to go to the company's store.

But he would have to go because his mother, knowing nothing, found it the most normal thing in the world to send him there, for flour, for needles, for boot polish. What could he say? I do not want to go to the store anymore? Boys go to the store. Fathers go to work in their uniforms. Mothers ask their boys to do things that are reasonable and normal.

When sons come home with blood on their faces, mothers wash them and sterilize the cuts with antiseptic fluid they bought at the company store. Then they ask what happened, and sons, being like fathers, do not tell any women such things.

The clerk at the store did not tell anyone, either. When the thief is the son of an officer, you manage to take care of the situation on the spot. You do not go to the army or the civil authority. You dispense a lesson just as you dispense the bottles filled with fluids for ailments. This boy had decided to steal for the second time, and it was a hot summer day on which the man in the stockroom of the store had experienced a toothache, was it? An earache?

In this country, as in the one everyone had come from, the grown men used their superior strength and experience to mete out punishment to the growing boys. It was generally considered that a boy who was considered generally to be a normal child of a respected family would learn his lessons about small crime by receiving physical punishment. When the grown male is suffering a toothache he might be more than usually enthusiastic about delivering the punishment.

The boy with the blood on his face keeps his part of the bargain by withholding the cause from his family. This was a sort of honour system that would be the basis for any kind of growing to be a man.

But he hated to go to the store. With the slanted scar beside his eye he hated to walk into the scene of last summer's lesson, especially when he entered to become the only person in the front room and he knew that the man was alone in the stockroom. Usually it passed through his mind that he might grab something and run, to bring himself up closer to even.

He had learned not to like thieves. Reading his Bible and listening to the homilies of his mother, he placed himself on the side of the honest. That was his problem now as he walked diagonally in the new snow. He wanted to steal something that would never be important to him, just to get up nearly to even.

Then another route suggested itself, just suggested it*self,* that he could see the *man's* blood. He walked in circles in the snow so that he would not even see that route.

This morning he had taken his mother's longest knife off its nail and cut bread with it. He had looked through the melting ice on the kitchen window toward the company's store, the knife in his hand. He had even put it under his shirt.

You want a good lesson, the man had said last summer.

Once in the autumn he had pulled his father's sword from its place and waved it in the light streaming in from the south window. He felt its edge and it was dull. His father explained ceremony and tradition to him, a kind of lesson that he knew was a very early step in preparing him for a responsible job in this colony, or more likely another.

So now he would stop making his shapes in the new snow and go to the store. He always lied to his mother and wondered whether that was another step outside the definition he had made for himself. He always told her that he could not remember everything he was supposed to get at the store. He asked her to write a list. He could hand the list to the man who came out of the stockroom and never have to say a word to him.

His father also had a pistol that he wore for ceremony and tradition, but he was an officer in the Royal Engineers. His weapons were a pencil and paper.

I sometimes wonder whether yours are. I have heard all that talk about imagination and invention, and frankly, it makes me wonder why you hide yourself behind an earlier century as you so often do. Of course I have heard all that cant about history's being the type of realist narrative and thus the perfect foil for anti-realist invention. That sounds a little forced to me.

I think that some people use history as a setting because they haven't the nerve to write in a world that they would have to present themselves in.

I also suspect that childhood is another version of history, that so many writers in North America especially write about young characters because they do not have to worry about their own vulnerability if the characters in their stories can be presented with the kind of irony that depends on children's supposed innocence and clarity.

I suppose that I may be suggesting that you drop all these masks and try to write about what you know. It is an old and perhaps discredited maxim, but in your case, it may be a place from which to start a frank enquiry into, what should we call it, life?

It was like this every year. He was walking around and around in the biggest department store in town. Well, it used to be the biggest department store in town. It was really no longer the biggest department store in town, but it was the oldest. It bore the name of the oldest private company in the world. Every year around the middle of winter he walked around and around in this store, hoping to see something that would answer a question he would like to get out of the way.

Every year he would manage to find a suitable present for his mother, but before he found it he would walk past numberless counters, deeper and deeper in annoying despair. He could not remember what he bought for her last year. He tried to imagine what she would be expecting. Maybe she would say it was enough for her that he drove all the way up there to see her again this Christmas. Maybe he bought her the same thing every year, and she was expecting another one.

He hated this store, but he thought it was so big that it must have something in it that he could buy. He walked past a pile of sweaters and for a moment held some material between his thumb and forefinger. The more he walked around this floor and then up the escalator, inwardly cursing the people who merely stood side by side waiting to be carried, and then around the floor above, the less he took notice of the details in the displays.

Inwardly, he cursed the somnambulant herds of Christmas shoppers. His body exaggerated his impatience as he sucked in his stomach and edged sideways between fat women in fur coats. He did not whisper apologies when he bumped into someone's packages. Inwardly, he cursed Christmas. He smiled ruefully, not for anyone else, when he thought of his sister. His sister did her shopping from mail order catalogues in August.

Whatever he bought would be short of satisfactory. But there had been a year, hadn't there, when he had bought the perfect present. He remembered feeling satisfied when his mother opened the present and let everyone know how really happy she was at last. But what was it? Well, even if he remembered what it was, he could not buy that present again.

When he was in grade three he got a wooden pistol that went *click*. He took his disappointment outside and did his best, pointing it at an apple tree and then at the side of his own head. In grade four he got a cartooning set and spent hundreds of hours with it, happily in touch with his long long future.

He longed for summer. No, he longed for early January, when it would be almost a year until the next Christmas. He hated being in this big old store. It looked a little sparse, a little *Russian* since the bigger department store had gone up across the street, kitty-corner. He had walked around in that store, too. But the hatred he felt in this store held something more than the hatred in that more crowded place. There was something old about the hatred he felt in this store. He had never been a boy in that other store. It was all designer blue jeans and famous-name basketball shoes. In this store you could still get company blankets.

When he was in grade eight a friend had walked out of this store with two standing ashtrays, just to show that it could be done if you looked all right. Afterward, he had helped his friend bring them back in and leave them just inside the south doors.

The floors were hard white tiles. If he slipped and fell he would make a great clatter and break a bone or two. Women's heels clacked and you could hear them because of the sparseness. He followed a woman with high heels and beautiful long legs for a while, but this was not getting his shopping done. His car rested somewhere underground, and by the time he found it, the parking fee would be something to consider. The sooner he bought something for his mother, the better.

Every Christmas made him want to throw things, to push things over. Maybe he should buy his mother some dishes. Yes, yes, her little house was full of dishes that wouldn't even be brought out on ceremonial occasions. A set of really sharp Japanese knives. Oh yes, she survived largely on a diet of toast and canned peaches. Upstairs somewhere, along a counter in a back corner of sporting goods, there was a display of rifles and shotguns, and crossbows. Better stay away from sporting goods.

Later in the week he would produce a series of drawings of his poor sad self going crazy in a department store, a moron never to learn a simple life skill. But now he was trying not to slip as he walked across the melted snow on the hard white tiles just inside the big south doors.

Two Glasses of Remy

I like to think of myself as an impulsive character. It seems more interesting, is what I mean to say. But I didn't usually do things like that, not actually do them.

We were in the left-hand lane, waiting for a green light, and the taxi was in the right lane. I could see her plain as day, or really it was eleven at night, and she was sitting over on the other side of the back seat, weeping her eyes out. It was the light on Cambie, so there was a long wait, usually hate getting caught at Cambie.

The cab driver wasn't paying any attention, just looking at the red, and there she was, this old lady, didn't even have a hankie, just bawling, not really bawling, just crying with her bony mouth open in the back of a Yellow Cab. I didn't even say anything to Willy, just opened my door and took two steps and opened the cab door and got in, just when the light went green. The cab driver didn't have time to react till he was moving. I didn't even look at Willy. He had to make his move before the people behind him got murderous. I don't know whether he drove along beside us or not.

Before I knew anything I had put my right arm around her shoulders, and she just put her grey head on my chest, half on my chest and half on my shoulder. Now the cabbie looked in his mirror and said, "What's happening?"

I said, "It's okay."

She was slowing down on the sobs.

"Ma'am?" said the cabbie.

"It's all right," she said. Her voice was a little weak, and there was crying in it. But the cabbie must have figured we knew each other.

"You still going the same place?" he asked.

"Yes," she said, no sob.

It was warm in the cab. Now I noticed her scent. I don't have any idea what I expected. I guess I usually think that old ladies either smell funny or they wear too much perfume, the kind your grandmother always left all over you after she gave you a little hold. But this old lady smelled terrific, with one of those slight aromas that remind you of herbs or trees. I started worrying about whether I smelled all right.

She was sort of thin and seemed pretty tall, and as far as I could tell, she was wearing an expensive fur wrap and some kind of suit thing or dress that might as well have been a suit, dark, made by a tailor. I could see the bottom halves of her legs in the faint light coming in off the streetlamps. She was wearing black stockings you could see through, and she had those great legs you sometimes see on old ladies when they're rich. She was letting all the weight of her upper body lean on me, her arms tucked in front of her and her head on my chest.

The taxi had been turning right and left. Now it turned left off Blanca, I guess, and into Belmont. These were all million dollar houses when a million dollar house was still something. The taxi turned in to a circular drive in front of a big white mansion, I guess you'd say. Now what, I thought. She took her time sitting up straight. I got out my wallet, but she was already handing the driver a bill and waving away the change. Was I going to ride away with the cab? The lady got out her side and left the door open and walked away toward the house. I slid across and got out, clumsy, and closed the door. The cab crunched away on the circle.

There were no lights on in the house. What was I supposed to do? This wasn't a pickup. She never asked me into the cab, and I didn't know what I was doing. She was crying, that's all, and I didn't know old ladies cried. I had to put my arm around her. I'm in my late thirties, well, forty. I don't jump into taxis.

But here we were at her house, or at least *a* house, a rich person's house. I'm not a gold digger, I'm not a gigolo, I'm a recently separated man with a taste for beer parlours and movies. Willy had been driving me home from the soccer game and a meatball sandwich on the Drive. Well, here I was, a short climb from the Fourth Avenue bus.

She was digging into her purse, and the fur wrap was hanging off one of her shoulders. I put it back right, and she smiled a tiny bit at me, tears in her eyes still, but no smudge. The driveway lights showed me a face that had once been very beautiful. Still was, in another way. I decided to walk her to her door, make sure she got in. I'll never tell this story to anybody, I decided.

But she had no intention of going to the enormous white door with the pillars in front of it. She aimed a little gizmo to the left, and one of the three garage doors went up. A lot of strange possibilities went almost through my head: Was I supposed to stay in the garage overnight? Was she giving me a car for being so nice? Was she a weird murderess with a garage full of ominous tools? She put a key chain into my hand, and walked on her straight legs into the garage. I followed her, of course—why deviate from my behaviour so far?

She was standing on the passenger side of a dark green Cadillac convertible with the top up. The garage lights were on. Beside the Caddy was a tan Rolls-Royce, and beside the Rolls was a black four-by-four of some sort. I couldn't leave a woman like her standing beside a Caddy door for long. There were about ten keys on the key ring. I had no idea what a Cadillac key looks like. While I tried four keys in her door she stood beside me. I was a hod carrier in the presence of superior breeding. But I managed to close the door for her with enough sophistication, I thought. And I got the driver's door open on the first try—no question of her leaning across to pop the handle.

I'd never driven a Cadillac before, and I'd never driven any kind of car during the year it was first bought. I was nervous about crunching something while backing out onto a circular driveway, but she just sat with her back and neck straight, looking straight ahead. I backed out, and before I found a forward gear, the garage light was out and the door was coming down. I could smell trees.

"Where to?" I asked, trying to sound casual or cheerful. She nodded. She probably had a gold tissue dispenser in the car or her purse, but she never dabbed at her eyes. I drove.

She didn't say anything while I took two rights and headed out the drive to the university. I could not hear the engine, only a wisp of tires on the wet pavement. We went past the Japanese garden and south along the ring road, the ocean to our right, beyond some trees that were made to look like a forest in a book for kids back on the prairies. That's how I think, even in situations where it's hard to think.

The rain clouds of the earlier evening were gone inland, and now the moon was up there, three-quarters full or a quarter empty. I reached for the radio, but she put her fingers on mine and left them there till I moved my hand back to the steering wheel. Then she had a cigarette in her hand. I reached for the Caddy's lighter, but this time she didn't touch me. Flame came out of something gold in her other hand, and I could smell French tobacco.

I cleared my throat and told her my name, sort of. From her silence with her cigarette, I knew she wasn't likely to give me hers. Instead, she motioned toward the lookout. This is a little parking space for about four cars. You can point the nose of your Toyota or Cadillac toward the edge of the cliff overlooking the Strait, and catch a glimpse of the log booms below. If you're in a Cadillac, your back bumper isn't all that far off the road. Down in the water there is supposed to be a famous sunken wreck.

She leaned toward me and I wondered what now, but she was after some gadget that retracted the roof. It went straight up and then back, and just disappeared. I was gawking. I'd never been in a Cadillac before. Maybe I was trying to persuade myself that the Cadillac convertible was the strange part of this event. She turned off the ignition and took the key out before a man's reassuring voice from the dashboard could finish telling her to. I decided that if we were going to talk, she was going to go first. It was not a warm night. There was a wind coming off the Strait, but she was wearing a fur stole. I turned my lapels out.

And we sat there, looking out to sea. There were a few lights on the water. A propeller plane descended toward the airport. I didn't turn my head, but I snuck a sideways look at her. The moonlight made her face look really nice. Not young or anything, but she had a long straight nose and straight hair that was tied loosely somehow at the back of her neck. The women her age that I know all have short hair done in curls. They don't go around crying in taxis.

Now she was opening the glove compartment, which in a Cadillac should be called an overcoat compartment. For the third time I saw moonlight moving in a big diamond ring, at least I thought it had to be a diamond, and now I could see what I thought I'd seen, that there was no gold band next to it. But now there were two heavy-looking whisky glasses and a bottle of Remy something, and she poured as if she were the barman at the Ritz, not a wasted motion, no hesitation, no clink.

For a while after my separation I had downed a few, but not one Remy anything. Lately I had stayed pretty well away from alcohol, but what would you do? I even took a French cigarette, though I had quit smoking again a month before. So we sat in a Caddy with the top down, smoking Gitanes and sipping extremely old brandy. Now that we had trees around us, I couldn't smell them anymore.

If you are sitting in the only automobile at a lookout around midnight, you are eventually going to pay attention to the woman sitting on the leather seat beside you, it doesn't matter what kind of woman. With a little warm brandy in my stomach, I gradually turned and looked at her. She was still facing toward the gleam on the sea, even while she jabbed her cigarette into the big ashtray. Maybe I should be ashamed of myself for looking her up and down, as they say, but I don't see why I should be. Her long grey hair was pulled back loosely, as I said, and except for a little strand that fell by her ear and moved in the wind, it looked as if it had been brushed with a silver-backed brush just a few minutes ago. The eye I could see was clear now. There were creases rather than wrinkles under her eye and near her mouth. She had not ruined her human beauty with a facelift, at least not recently. She held her chin high, as if she always did, and there was a little turkey in her neck, but not much, the amount you'd like to see in your mother or a politician. Her dress, because now I knew it was not a suit, was dark, and darker under the midnight moon, but

I could see that she was not scrawny or boardlike, pardon me
for using such words. She had medium-size breasts still. Now
her legs were crossed, and I could see her right leg from the
knee down. I have hardly ever seen a nicer leg. I was not turned
on, as people say, but I was surely impressed. I've been
married once, and I've been with a few people of the female
persuasion before and after. Well, during, too. But I have never
sat in a car or anywhere else with such a beautiful woman.
Lady, some people might say. If that sounds peculiar, I can't
help it. I like to think of myself as an experienced character,
but this woman who was now pouring a second Remy for us
made me feel like a boy in a bedtime story or something. I
don't mean anything by bedtime, let's say a fairy tale. Or let's
just drop that altogether.

This time there were no cigarettes, and I was glad about
that. When your first cigarette after a month is one of those
thick French ones with no filter, you get a little woozy. The
brandy eased my throat and made me look at the moon. It was
everywhere, in the clear sky, on the otherwise invisible water,
and on the smooth hood of the quiet car. It was in my head. If
that sounds romantic, why don't you try it sometime?

She put her glass with some brandy in it down on the open
door of the big glove compartment, and turned at last to look
at me. She took my glass and put it beside hers. For the first
time I could see her teeth, the ones in front. They were not
movie teeth, but they were very good. The tooth part of her
face was a little farther forward than it is with the average
person, something I've always liked, especially in women.

And now she smiled for about a second. I felt as if she was not smiling at me, and not because she was happy. That second's smile reminded me of the thing I'd seen in the taxi.

For the first time that I had noticed, she looked right into my eyes, and she did this for a while. In the moonlight she had a white face and deep black eyes, and then they were coming closer to me. She put her gentle bony fingers on the sides of my head, leaned way over on me, and kissed me on the mouth. Her mouth was open, and so was mine, in surprise. Electricity went through my body in a big car. She did something with her tongue for only one second, but she held the kiss. I could feel her breast against me, and as God is my witness, I considered touching it with my hand.

Then she was back where she had started, sitting upright, looking at the blessed ocean, her drink lifted to her lips. My heart was pounding, of all things, and I just couldn't reach for my glass. For a length of time I couldn't tell you, I looked straight in front of me, too. I tried to concentrate on visualizing the gears there on the cliff, where D was, where R was. I wanted to say something, but I couldn't, until she put her glass down empty and made the smallest sigh you can imagine. Maybe it was the kind of sigh you make when you finish a very old brandy.

"Can I ask you a question?" I said.

"May I," she corrected me, her voice closer than I would have expected.

"May I ask you a question?"

"One."

"Why were you crying in the taxi?"

I had to wait for her answer. Maybe she did, too.

"Because of you," she said at last.

"What?"

"That's two questions," she said.

She handed me my drink, and I finished it. I passed the glass back, but she did not take it from my hand. I put it on the glove compartment door, and then she put it away and closed the door. She picked the keys up and gave them to me. I turned on the ignition and concentrated on R. While I drove with the top down slowly back along the road between the trees, she took a little telephone from her purse and called Yellow Cab. She asked for a taxi at Belmont Drive and Blanca. I *will* get home tonight, I thought, or maybe I said it.

A SHORT STORY

It was that slightly disappointing moment in the year when the cherry blossoms have been blown off the trees, or shrunken to brown lace out of which little hard green pebbles are beginning to appear. The orchardists were running tractors between rows of trees, disking the late spring weeds into the precious topsoil left there by the glacier that long ago receded from the desert valley.

Starlings were growing impatient with the season, tired of competing with the season, tired of competing for scraps behind the Safeway store in town, eager for those high blue days when the cherries would be plump and pink, when they could laugh at the sunburnt men in high gumboots, who would again try to deceive them with fake cannons and old shirts stretched between the branches.

High over Dog Lake a jet contrail was widening and drifting south. The orchards on the west bank were in shadow already, and sunlight sparkled off windows of the new housing development on the other shore. The lake was spotted with brown weeds dying underwater, where the newest poison had been dumped by the government two weeks before.

Evening swallows were already dipping and soaring around the Jacobsen house, nabbing insects in their first minutes of activity after a warm day's sleep. The house was like many of the remodelled orchard homes in the southern part of the valley, its shiplap sides now covered with pastel aluminum, metallic screen doors here and there, a stone chimney marking the outside end of the living room. Fifteen years ago the living room had been used only when relatives from other valley towns came to visit. Now it was panelled with knotty cedar, animal heads looking across at one another from the walls, and the Jacobsens sat there after all the evening chores were done, watching Spokane television in colour, and reading this week's paper, or perhaps having some toast and raspberry jam.

The rug was a pastel shade fairly close to that of the outside surface. The Jacobsens lived with it, though neither of them particularly liked it. One of them had, once, when it was new; the other never thought of offering an opinion, or holding one.

CHARACTERS

The Jacobsens did not discuss things. They spoke short sentences to one another in the course of a card game, or while deciding which rerun was more worth watching on the mammoth television set parked under a deer head on the west wall of the living room.

"We haven't seen this Carol show, have we?" suggested Mrs. Jacobsen. "I think it must have been on the night we played bridge with Stu and Ronnie."

"No, we saw it," said Mr. Jacobsen from behind his sixteen-page newspaper. "This is the one where her and Harvey are on the jet plane that gets hijacked to South America."

"Skyjacked."

"The same thing. But if you want to watch it again, go ahead."

"I can't remember a skyjack one."

"Go ahead. I'll probably fall asleep in the middle, anyway," said Mr. Jacobsen.

Art Jacobsen was tired every night. As soon as the after-supper card game was over, and his short legs were up on the aquamarine hassock, his eyes would begin to droop. He was sixty-one years old and still working eleven hours a day in the orchard. Like most valley orchardists, he wore a shirt only during the early hours of the morning, when the dew was still on every leaf. His body was tanned and muscled, but it was getting more rectangular every year.

Audrey Jacobsen was ten years younger. She had only recently taken to colouring her hair, often a kind of brownish red she mistakenly remembered from her youth. Her first husband used to tease her about having red hair, though it wasn't true. By the time that Ordie Michaels had died and Art

Jacobsen had started courting her on rainy days, her hair was a good plain brown, usually under a kerchief.

She'd taken to wearing the kerchief, as all the women did, while sorting fruit at the Co-op Packing House. By the time Donna was five, Audrey had assumed the habit of wearing it all the time, except when she went for drives with Art Jacobsen.

They had been watching Carol on television for five years now, and she didn't know whether she liked the show.

POINT OF VIEW

It is not that I know all about the Jacobsens and Donna Michaels before I start telling you about them. I am what they call omniscient, all right, but there isn't any Jacobsen family until I commit them to this medium. I have some hazy ideas or images, rather, or their story, a sort of past and a present, I suppose, but really for me the story is waiting somewhere in the future. Or I should say that I'm waiting for a time in the future when I will have the time to come to it, here. As a matter of fact, you don't have to, now, wait as long for it as I do.

So I am in the position ascribed to the narrator with the totally omniscient point of view. A know-it-all. Don't you believe it! God-like. Don't you believe it!

For instance, I've been thinking about writing this story for two years. Just a month ago I began to imagine a woman visiting her mother and stepfather at their orchard home, and that common emotional violence later on. But I just got the names while I was writing the first parts of the story, and I didn't imagine the Jacobsen house near the lake—I thought it would be forty kilometres farther south.

Do I have to mention that there is something difficult to explain about a third-person omniscient narrative having all these I's in it? Point of view dictates distance. Well, I would like to keep you closer than your usual "god" will allow (except for people such as yourself, Leda) (no, that's not what I'm trying to do to you, reader; don't be so suspicious).

From up here I can see the Jacobsen house as a little square surrounded by trees that have nearly lost their blossoms and are just producing leaves. I have good eyes; I need them to see all that through the drifting jet contrail.

By the way, have you noticed that when the narrator speaks in the first person, he makes you the second person? When he speaks of others in the third person, you are perhaps standing beside him, only the parallax preventing your seeing exactly what he is seeing. That makes for a greater distance produced by the first person narrative. You must have noticed that.

PROTAGONIST

Donna Michaels, an attractive honey blonde in her early twenties, was about four kilometres from the Jacobsen house, driving along the lakeside road in her dented Morris Minor convertible. She had already gone through her rite of passage between innocent childhood and knowledgeable maturity, involving strong Freudian implications. Now she was driving through a warm valley evening, wishing that she had come a week ago when the cherry blossoms were still at the beginning of their decline.

She had not been home during blossom time for seven years, and perhaps this more than anything else told her that she had really ceased to be a valley kid, that she was a coast person. Looking to her right, she could see, even in the shadows made by the hills over the water, splotches of brown weeds under the surface of the lake. A part of her that still wanted to be a valley person was hurt by that.

She thought about taking a Valium before she got there, only two kilometres to go now. It was not really the time to appear. She should have arrived while Art was still out in the orchard so she could have a calm talk with her mother. When Art was there, making his blustery remarks or criticisms about her language, her mother could be depended on to remain silent, just as she had always done during family hassles, just as she had done then.

"I love him, Donna. What am I supposed to do?" she had said.

"More than you love me?" That newcomer.

"I *chose* him."

That was the last time her mother had ever said anything so devastatingly open.

She got out of the car and took a Valium. One gets adept at swallowing them without water. She was mildly surprised that she was walking slowly toward the single little ponderosa pine that used to be her going-to-be-alone place in the far corner of their orchard. It had perhaps grown four inches taller. Looking farther up, she could see Star Bright. She made a trivial wish and walked slowly back to the dusty car.

What a beautiful sight she was, with her long legs and summer dress, sunglasses perched on top of her short feathery blondish hair.

SYMBOLISM

Donna got back into the dented Morris Minor, and before she let the clutch out, she unaccountably thought about the animal heads protruding from her stepfather's walls. The first time she had seen one, she had gone to the room next door to see whether the elk's body stuck out from that side. What had been done with the bodies? she wondered now. Were they discarded, left on the forest floor for the delectation of the ants? Did the family eat them? She couldn't remember eating mountain goat or moose, and she had been a picky eater as a child.

She decided that whatever had been done with the torso and legs, Art was only really interested in the trophy. He talked about nature a lot, but he was quite comfortable under the stare of the big glass eyes.

When she was twelve, her dog Bridey passed away after a fit. Quickly, before he would have a chance to take her to the taxidermist, Donna put the heavy and limp body along with an adult's shovel into a wheelbarrow and pushed it for half an hour through the crumbling earth to the ponderosa. There she wasted no time looking at Bridey's fur and tight-closed eyes. She dug a hole and dropped her in and covered her up, without looking. She left no marker. She knew where Bridey was, and that was all that was necessary.

Now, she reflected, looking at the sagebrush growing around her tree, they probably knew too, he probably saw the wheel tracks the next morning.

She let out the clutch and drove the last kilometre slowly, having pulled on the lights. Just in time, a mother quail and her five little ones raced in a line to the safety of the roadside weeds. She smiled as she imagined the mother there, counting them.

Then she was at the turn just before their driveway, where the truck and the new Toyota were parked in a sharp vee. People here along Rawleigh Road never pulled their drapes. Through the window she could see Mr. and Mrs. Jacobsen, an over-coloured Carol, and a deer she used to call Bambi, first childishly, then later to needle her stepfather.

Her car's wheels crunched over the driveway. Before she got out she did up her two top buttons.

CONFLICT

Donna had driven four hundred kilometres to be there, but she didn't want to go inside the house. Of course in a setting such as this, they would know that somebody had driven up the gravel driveway, and one of them, probably her mother, would be walking to the door at this moment.

Donna wanted to be with her mother, especially because she never wrote letters home. She did not even imagine writing

"Mrs. A. Jacobsen" on an envelope. She felt as if, yes, she still loved her mother, that strange older woman in polyester slacks, though they had not once spoken to each other on the telephone since Jacobsen had mounted her as his casual season's trophy. What ambiguity in the delivery of the thought. When it was accomplished, and all three knew, what depressing decisions and solitudes.

Donna could not stay in that family where her first love, her first world face, lost all hope and fell in, decided to stay with the bringer of death. What polluted language in the formerly unchallenged eden. Why? How, rather.

"But I chose him. I made my choice."

"Do you love him? Can you?"

"I chose him."

She was not a woman then, but she was not a valley girl, either. She left Dog Lake, she had to, and there was no question but the city on the coast, several ruinous jobs, and some solitary education.

Now the door opened and it was Audrey who was illuminated by the porch light. Donna was momentarily ashamed with disappointment that her mother, Mrs. Michaels, was not the picture of a defeated lustreless farm wife, the sensitive buffeted by life, such as one expected to find in the Canadian novels she had been reading.

"Donna! For the Lord's sake! Why didn't you tell us you were coming? Come in, you rascal," the woman said, her arms outstretched as if offering the red knitting she had been doing while watching television.

Donna held her mother's elbows and kissed her nose as she felt the screen door bat against her rear. Her mother chattered with a little confusion as the pretty blonde deposited her purse and a book and something wrapped in party paper on the telephone table.

"Well, well," said Art Jacobsen, looking up from his paper, his feet still stretched out on the hassock.

DIALOGUE

"I wish I'd gotten here while the blossoms were in full bloom," said Donna. It was the perfect little bit of business to get through the awkwardness of their surprise.

"Oh, we had a wonderful year for blossoms," said her mother. "When a breeze came up, the whole valley smelled like a garden."

"It *is* a garden," said Donna, getting herself a cup of coffee from the pot on the stove. She came back through the arch into the living room, where her mother was still standing with the knitting in her hands. "At least that's how we coast people think of it."

Art shook his paper to a new page.

"It's not the blossoms that count. It's the bees."

"The workers, you mean," said Donna, a little edge on her voice. She sat down with her coffee, not looking at him.

"Yeah, the queen sits at home, getting fatter and fatter, while the workers bring her the honey," said Art, his eyes looking at a news photo of the local skeet-shooting champs.

"Have you had any supper, dear?" Audrey piped in.

"Yes, I stopped at the Princeton bus station cafe, for old times' sake," said Donna.

That was a nice shot. It was there that she had abandoned Art's truck that night, with the keys in the dash. She'd taken the bus to Vancouver with no baggage, not even clean underwear. Just two apples and her purse.

Art didn't say a word now.

"Well, well," said Audrey Jacobsen.

There was a silence. Even the knitting needles crossed and opened without a sound. It was pitch dark outside. A mirrored deer looked in from between two young Lombardy poplars.

"How are all your aches and pains, Mom?" Donna asked at last, idly looking at snapshots from a glass bowl on the table beside her chair. Carol was over, and Art raised his remote control and shot the set off.

"Oh, the osteopath in Penticton said I did something to my lower spine when I was a girl, and I can never expect to be 100 percent."

"Does that mean you're not all there?" asked Art.

FLASHBACK

When he seemed absolutely ready to give it up, give up on it, to settle for some costly talk then, she offered him a cigarette, which he took politely, and lit one herself. It was the only sort of occasion upon which she smoked anything.

They were always grateful, the talkers, when she by her gestures allowed them a certain comfort, a freedom from embarrassment.

"Thank you," he had said, and lay on his back beside her, carefully sharing the ashtray she kept on her belly.

"You needn't feel badly." Her voice was soft and sure, caring and casual, it seemed. "You might be surprised how often it happens. You had a lot to drink, I would imagine, it was only enough to make you think you wanted me. Happens quite a lot."

"No, that's not it. Well, it might be a little, but that's not really it. It's. . . ."

She did not offer the interruption he was waiting for. She just smoked her cigarette. She butted it out in the ashtray, and handed the ashtray to him. So he had something to do with his free hand.

"It's just that you are about exactly the age of my daughter," he said.

"No kidding," she said, with a twiggy edge to her voice, and that was his first hint that it was time to go back to his hotel.

FORESHADOWING

After he had left, she got the scissors and clipped her toenails. Having done five, she lay back and imagined the john walking back to his hotel. He did not seem like the taxi-taking kind.

She pictured him lying on her, brought by her to the

margin of success. Then she yanked the scissors toward her, fetching a jolt as they sank into the flesh of his back. It was not an old movie on midnight television. The points of her scissors were just below the joining of her ribcage, forcing the skin a little.

I wonder whether I could just throw a few clothes into the car and drive to Montreal, she thought.

Maybe you could work your way across the country, she replied.

She clipped five toenails again. They were the same ones.

PLOT

The spare bedroom of the Jacobsen house was also a kind of storeroom. It contained a gun rack in which one could find a pump-action shotgun, a .22-calibre repeater rifle, an old .303 that once belonged to the Canadian Army, a .44 handgun in a tooled holster, a 30-30 with a scope sight, and a collector's .30-calibre machine gun with a plugged barrel. This is where Donna was, taking off her light cardigan and shoes, finding the toothbrush and dental floss in the bottom of her big-city street bag, looking at herself, untanned, in the vanity mirror. A severed goat head looked over her shoulder.

Through two walls she could hear the Jacobsens disputing. Art's voice rose and rose, and at the end of a declarative sentence fragment it uttered the word "slut," followed by an exclamation point.

One would expect the ammunition to be locked up, and it was, in a cabinet with glass-panel doors. Donna shook the pillow out of one of the pillowcases, wrapped the pillowcase around her fist, and punched one of the glass panels three times, each time with greater force.

The male voice rose to the word "hell" and stopped. A door banged against a wall, and heavy footsteps approached. Donna threw the pillowcase onto the bed beside her sweater. When Art propelled the bedroom door open, Donna was pointing a loaded shotgun at his head.

Art backed out of the bedroom and walked backward all the way to the living room. There he observed a slight movement of the dark holes he had wiped clean just the night before, and sat down in his favourite chair. He was on top of Audrey's knitting, but he felt convinced that he should not bring attention to such a minor problem.

Audrey Jacobsen, usually a chatterbox, found it hard to find the words she should say.

She said, "Donna. . . ."

It was frightening that Donna did not say a word. Art looked depressed. He was a heavy man in his chair. Donna blew out her breath.

"For God's sake, girl, that's my husband!"

Donna did not breathe in.

"He's my husband. He's all I have!"

Donna turned a smooth quick arc and shot her mother's face off.

THEME

Donna walked from the house and into the orchard, the shotgun still dangling. She had no shoes on. No one followed her, and she did not look behind. She was walking between two rows of cherry trees, so that when a quick hard breeze came around a rock outface it blew a snow of exhausted blossoms over her head.

Donna walked down the slope, not flinching when a clacking sprinkler spun slowly and soaked her dress from the waist down. It was really dark out now, and she could see the lights of the retirement village on the far side of the lake.

The gun had made a dreadful noise. But now the night life was speaking again, crickets nearby and frogs from down by the lake. They were calling each other to come and do it.

Donna walked till she came to the dirt road with the row of couch grass down the middle and followed it till she arrived at her ponderosa. There she sat down with her back to its narrow trunk and dropped the shotgun to the dry ground. The sky was filled with bright stars that seemed to have edges, and black behind them. One never saw anything like that from the streets in Vancouver. She thought of the universality speaking through her condition.

Nearby, her dog curled, waiting for Donna to signal something to her. But Donna ignored her, as she fought to remember what had happened in the last hour, or was it some years? An airline jet with powerful landing lights appeared from the other side of the hills and descended over the lake, heavily pulling back on its fall toward the airstrip at the end.

Now that her eyes were adjusted to the late spring darkness of the valley, she saw a bat flipping from direction to direction above her. She remembered the fear that it might get caught in your hair. Bats don't get caught in your hair.

I'm not very old, Donna thought. I'm not very old and here I am already. She picked up the shotgun and fired the other barrel, and threw it over the side of the hill.

The Creator Has
a Master Plan

T hey were in a twenty-six-dollar room at the Chelsea Hotel in cement Manhattan. She was lying on the bed, her hair in curlers under a bandanna.

Little flag of disposition, as at the *novillero* bullfight in Mexico City five years earlier he had resolutely bought seats in the sun.

Reading a book on *Blow Up* they had found earlier in the afternoon. Just lying there in the middle of Nueva York as if they were moving in and there was no hurry to do anything but rest. The brown dresser had been painted numerous times and cream-yellow showed under the brown where some predecessor had moved something.

He was standing beside it, wiggling his fingers, and were they going to see any roaches? She was also smoking a new cigarette, he had seen her that way thousands of times, lying

89

on a bed, head on pillows, smoking a cigarette and reading a book, in the one hotel where they had given up worrying about that. Thomas Wolfe should fall off a fire escape? No sense worrying about that. But here in the middle of lower Manhattan and not walking anywhere in the early evening, even given the cold wet wind, manhole covers flush with the cement ring out when your heel hits them in late December.

I mean it was cold. New York City cold? Movies and stories got pictures of Harlem kids with their bums turned to the gush of free city water from the fire hydrant, childless taxi drivers with shirts unbuttoned over cotton singlets on Seventy-second Street.

She was reading the book, reading the book. She was interested in Antonioni all right, in fact that was her favourite movie, but she had had herself done up, she was waiting for tonight. That's why they weren't at least walking around the Village this afternoon, not in curlers, you go ahead if you want to, dear. She was also not going to go with him to Slugs' Bar, to hear Pharaoh and his brash new group, African some-thing, and he didn't know, but he knew, where she was going, to see him at the convention hotel, three thousand miles from where he lived now, presumably still with his wife who never went on "these trips" with him. Reading a book and waiting for that.

The reason for coming to New York was to be in the city, to add that, and reading that what's-in-town page of *The New Yorker* to find out that Pharaoh was at Slugs', that was a bonus. But more than that, to bring her with him, to the convention he would not attend, Honey, just being with you in the automat. Sure, he had seen *Blow Up,* like everyone else more than once, and it was a good movie, or film, rather, but there is time for that back home. But I can't remember now, did I see any tennis balls?

Won't you come out for a walk, see Washington Square? Henry James? Maxwell Bodenheim?

No, you go ahead, I need a rest.

A rest from or a rest for, he thought, and okay see you later, he took the old cage elevator out, and what did he do if not buy a *Times* and read the hockey scores at the nearest corned beef counter.

There she is, in the middle of NYC, he thought, my *enamorata* in a room on Twenty-third Street where Thomas Wolfe once laid his long frame. All alone, for now, I can go and then thread these streets in search of her, climb the fire escape or pretend my instinct takes me unerringly through unremembered halls, and knock excitedly at that door. I brought her to New York, thousands of miles over a half-dozen years, and her only distance is the twenty-five blocks to his hotel, the fancy one, where famous scholars recline.

He felt as if he had lived here once, in a portion of his life now blanked from recall by surgery he also could not remember. It was a bright cold day, the air of cement city full of desalinated water. The sun fell in rectangles on pavement repaired a hundred times and compressed heavier than any surface he'd ever seen. They had both come from towns where shepherd's thumb grew between the blacktop and the sidewalk. In the paper there was somebody worried about handsome Rod Gilbert's spinal fusion.

He did walk alone to Washington Square. There inside the ruined ring he saw the only snow in town, grey-white, almost water, tracked with oozing footprints. Everybody was indoors, bellied to the bar in Eisenhower jackets. He didn't need one but he decided for a drink, he would find the Third Street bar he'd read so much about. The famous poet would be there, he'd memorized the address. "Most men go down to obliteration / with the homeliest of remembrances." He walked around and around, coming always within three blocks according to the number, but never found it, running time and again into the facade of the downtown university. Well, he had other addresses in his book. He decided to forget them. If it can beat me the first time, I'm not going to make a fool of myself again. A fool to whom? Rod Gilbert, also from Quebec, rode on top of this town, in a velour armchair on the thirtieth floor. Everyone he saw lived here, secure in their language, safe inside the numbers assigned to the hard furrows cut across the cement island.

It was enough to be here, then. Seeing everything would not add anything to the collection. It is there in the booklet, like Duluth, let's say, and for instance El Paso.

He strode, in the wind, wearing his red toque with the mask rolled up inside, his many-coloured electrician gloves on, unattractive but interesting talismans, his green-and-black-checked woollen shirt, City of Westminster policeman's cape, winter-time boutique slacks, expensive Spanish boots with the deft square toes, proud of his small feet. Looking down at them, he saw a finger on the pavement, quickly, Twelfth Street, flush against the sidewalk.

It was one of those wonderful ideas that come along occasionally, usually when you're comfortable but tired, and distracted by someone else's uninteresting narrative. But there it was, really, a white man's finger in the gutter. It looked like a forefinger. Wouldn't it be interesting to take it back to the hotel and say see, look what you miss by just lying waiting for your familiar and designated tryst. But he wouldn't, he knew, pick such a thing up, even with his stained gloves on. A few years ago, he liked to think, he would have, but he also knew, walking away, that he wouldn't have.

He was after all a visitor in town. There was no one he wanted to phone at headquarters, and it was just three inches of grey flesh in New York. Why, that is, even bother to wonder how it got there? One learns the politics of a place by effort, not by accidents.

They did have dinner together, anyway, in an overheated restaurant two steps down from the cold wet late afternoon. He never noticed the name of the place and didn't have anything to eat he could not have got at home. He told her about his failure to find the bar, but not about the find he did make. He was chattering slowly, putting off hearing what she was going to say, and giving her time to think about how she was going to say it, how she would say no she didn't want to go and hear his music, that's not what she came to New York for, and certainly not that place. Or if he was willing, she wouldn't have to say the rest at all, how she was going to be in mid-Manhattan, seeing him who had been there so easily so often before, the expert and highly ranked star in the profession her husband had fallen back upon for security and for her.

The conference was called for the Modern Language Association but this was probably a story told since the dawn of time. He said to himself I'm here in New York anyway, distracted by that abruption, I'll have Pharaoh for the first time live, the newest language in this city, I can gather up the continued story after our trip back to the other island city.

So it was. Now he was on Third Street, east of Avenue D, his electrician gloves holding back little of the imagined East River cold, his heartbeat either palpable or audible, looking for the place he'd read about on record jackets, looking for a sign.

All the innocent bystanders were inside somewhere having something done to them by the outside agitators. He had never expected the street to look like this, not even in the dark—it was more fitting in his mind for a small town that had never attained any finish, any gloss. There were none, no signs, just paintless storefronts, most of them looking like a shut-down mining town, plywood nailed over windows, once in a while a door of plywood and tin patches that looked as if it might open for what business inside, black people with unpressed gabardine slacks, in one of them they were playing pool. There were mounds on the sidewalk. He had to step into the street to get around a charred mattress. There was nearly of a certainty a discarded body behind one of these buildings, with parts missing, a wedding band that wouldn't slip off. But he was a tall man with work boots laced around the top, or so he remembered it. In the darkest part of Manhattan he walked. It must have been neater when Hart Crane was here. There was a dull street lamp about a block and a half ahead.

And just after it a nameless place with sound for a change inside. Slugs' Bar on Tuesday night. He went, white as a sheet with a pointed top, in. It was crowded, first night, hundreds of black people in ordinary clothes, this was December 1968, and he took his toque off before he went to the bar. He got a small beer in a thin-bottomed American glass, the music all the time in his ears, and there was one chair to sit in so he asked with his eyes and it was okay and he sat. He wanted to look as if he was used to Pharaoh's music, which he was, and used to being here, which he was not. No one noticed, so his head followed his ears to the music and then he was surprised, pleasantly, he was at last thrilled. The chair was just an old wood-and-cane chair but at last he was sitting down in New York.

Now let's concentrate on this surprise. Pharaoh usually back home on the other concrete island, from the stereo in the living room alcove, played a tenor saxophone like a voice saying let me in. Here the horn was not in sight and that's what he'd come here looking for, the instrument of that sound that had unnerved her and made him know that the horn was not immediately a "musical instrument," it was a way of speaking and he had for himself only a way of listening. Now here on the stage it wasn't Joe's Jazz Club quintet, dark suits and cool dark faces and one pair of horn-rims. They were banging things together, making swellings of African banging sound, long and sweet, wearing orange and black Afric duds. Pharaoh leaned his little body against a post and slapped two tambourines together, looked like cymbals, sounded like the piece-by-piece concentration of making new music for a new village set into a cleared place on the forest floor.

Well, do we really have to try to describe music?—go listen to *Karma,* Impulse AS-9181. There were more bodies arriving, more chairs brought from somewhere, occasionally a waitress and another small beer, his body shifted, he agreeably and unconsciously reached down with his fingers and hopped his chair closer to the next, making room. The wall of music and the wall of bodies, thickening.

So it went on, evening east of Avenue D, more bodies in the dark, smoke drifting into the light on the stage, music beating into his flesh, and he was so happy and so lonely it was just right, somewhere. A singer he didn't know was yodelling in a fashion invented for the purpose, something he had never heard but it was intended to vocalize Africa. His name was Leon and so he reigned, there. The American beer was thin but it was cold, and in his other hand he held a Canadian cigarillo. He had no idea how he would get back to the Wolfe hotel but presumed he would walk, through the cement gauntlet, take a bang on his red hat. But now was now, not time but occurrence, not beat but interval. Another hand was presently lying on his thigh. He moved his knee slightly from side to side once. Would that mean fear or encouragement?

And to himself, what? The hand moved, assuredly, finger by finger, up his leg. He watched Pharaoh the tiny man looking with satisfaction at the success of this totally new American music, and it was old, older than the rotted piles in the East River. Now the zipper was slid easily and his flesh was in that hand so soon. He actually took a sip of beer as he came hard and God knows where on the back of a chair and as he felt the last ministrations of that hand he wondered, is it female or is it male, was it white or was it black? And as always happened in his life, he rose and left, unbelievably smoothly through that dense crowd of knees. A few minutes later he was walking, north on Avenue D.

There was a wet flaky snow. It fell and melted on the shoulders of his black woollen cape and on his knitted cap. He walked up the wide finger of Manhattan wondering how long he would remain alive this late at night here in the river dark. He felt as if his electrician gloves would protect him, something too—*outré*—for the spectators in the shadows.

To entertain himself till he got to Twenty-third Street, he composed the conversation they would have back in the little room if she was there. She would say they got stuck in the elevator coming down from the suite in the midtown hotel. He would say he got into a fistfight with someone he couldn't see in the dark and the falling snow. And it would go on from there.

LITTLE ME

Three times a week I have my early afternoon meal at Daphne's Lunch, an ordinary place frequented by the less affluent workers of the neighbourhood and by the widows who live in the high-rise apartments nearby. They know me there, and call me by my first name. In return I generally have the daily special. Today it was chicken soup and a patty melt. At Daphne's Lunch they make good soup and pretty bad patty melts.

I always take something with me to read, sometimes a magazine like *Saturday Night,* but usually a book. They know me as the guy who is always reading, I suppose, and not the garbagy drugstore paperbacks some of the shop girls open in front of their salads. Today I was about halfway through *Running in the Family* by Michael Ondaatje.

Always reading. Nevertheless I notice the fellow diners around me. It is a place for regulars. There is the fat old lady with the enormous bun of hair atop her head and the cigarette holder clenched between her teeth. She looks like Roosevelt when she lifts her chin. There is the couple that always sits in the dead-centre booth. I have never heard him utter a sound, and I have never seen him meet anyone's eyes. He just sits there and eats his plain burger and drinks two cups of tea. His wife, or such I presume her to be, never stops talking. Not talking, exactly; rather, she issues a constant stream of whispered curses between her nearly meeting teeth. She has yellowish white hair that she never washes but just pins back in sticky rectangles.

There are lots and lots of regulars. I never say hello to any of them. I am the sort of person who has to be introduced, and who soon forgets names if he is introduced. I do talk with the waitresses, and even get to know some of their names. If I get to know a name, I use it in a little bit of friendly fooling before I order the special. Once I ordered a toasted chicken salad sandwich instead of the daily special, and Delores had a hard time believing me.

Today I saw some people I had never seen before. Two of them I don't remember well at all. They were two young women enjoying Daphne's famous old-fashioned milkshakes in the can. The third person was an infant, I suppose you would call him, in a stroller. They had him parked at the open end of their booth, which was right across from mine.

I always look at children. If they are young enough I start an interchange with them. I offer winks and smiles and stuck-out tongues, and receive in return grins and stares, and once in a while a comic grimace.

So I looked at this child.

He was staring at me. Completely still, hardly blinking, with large serious eyes quietly open, he stared at me. And I was staring, I am sure, at him. Anyone watching us would think we were having a staring contest, a little child and a fifty-year-old man.

I usually don't stare. Over all the years I have managed to develop a technique of seeing enough without staring. But on this occasion I was probably staring. I was certainly not doing the usual thing—looking away and then after a while, back and then away again. I was looking at this preternaturally quiet kid.

Or maybe I wasn't. Maybe I was looking at something more familiar. I say this seemingly pointless thing for this reason: the kid had my face.

I am not saying that an eighteen-month-old child had a wrinkled old guy's face. But he did not have an eighteen-month-old's face either. He had the large head and open face of a boy about six years old. He had the face I wore when I was six years old. I have seen that face hundreds of times in photographs, and since this afternoon I think I can remember seeing it in my grandmother's living room mirror.

I had a high forehead, large brown eyes, straight brown hair that lay diagonally across my brow, large front teeth with a gap between the two top ones in front. A large face with solemn innocence on it. I was looking at it for the first time in four and a half decades.

I left half of my patty melt and went home, forgetting to go to the supermarket. That is all right, though. It is far past dinnertime and everyone around here seems to have fended for themselves. I seem to have forgotten to eat altogether.

JUNE 18, 1988

I don't generally go to Daphne's Lunch two days in a row, but I was there today. Despite my resolve, I had a cheeseburger and fries, with HP Sauce on the fries. I picked up that trick years ago, hoping the HP Sauce would keep my friend Artie away from my fries. It didn't work, and I found out that I liked it on my fries.

But what am I doing going on about HP Sauce? I rather suspect that I went to Daphne's Lunch to see whether that child with my face might show up again. I thought that I might have a look from another angle, with different weather and sky outside, in the middle of another kind of mood. I was thinking that I might fail to see the resemblance today.

I was rather hoping that, you might imagine. But I was also curious to have another look at my young face. If he still did look exactly like me at six or seven, I wanted to see more. I don't know what I was planning to do about it. It would not do to approach the child's mother and ask her where she got him.

But one feels that one might do something. I felt peculiar every time I remembered that face last night. I felt, I think, a little afraid. Nervous, at least. I do not often consult books about my feelings. I refuse to consider anything to do with astrology, C. G. Jung, or blood sugar. But I thought I would see what I could find about one's double—as long as I did not have to go outside of the house to find such references. As long as it was literary references I was looking at.

Well, I found out that we have a library full of double stories. They all wrote them, not just Joseph Conrad and Dostoyevsky and Robert Louis Stevenson. They all did. Literature seems, once you start looking, to be filled more than anything else with twins, shadows, mirrors, schizophrenia, robots, puppets, voodoo dolls, and so on and on. Every society has double stories, and every age group has them. They mean a lot of different things, depending on whether the stories are about sex or religion or madness.

How lucky I am! I can have an unsettling experience in a greasy spoon and simply look into my book room at home to reassure myself about it. One writer tells us this: that the double is not only strange, but also very familiar, because he was once within us. Another warns that we mess around with doubles at our peril because of the risk of being dominated by them. Still another cautions about a crisis of identity.

I learned after about fifteen minutes to skip through most of the stuff I was encountering. I kept seeing, as if they were staring up through the pages, the wide calm eyes of that infant with the child's face so familiar to my parents.

Oh, it was just one of those things, a fluke of lighting. Taking advantage of my distraction or tiredness. I have been having a hard time getting used to my new glasses. I wouldn't mind seeing the kid again, but it was just a lot of kaka.

Still, I wish that the usual idea about the appearance of the *doppelgänger* was something different. If you see it you are supposed to get ready to die.

But really, a *doppelgänger* is a twin, a creature or appari-
tion the same size and age as oneself. There aren't any little
kid *doppelgängers* for grown-ups.

JUNE 20, 1988

They were there again today, the kid and his mother. She had
the same friend with her as before. They were both wearing
plastic jackets. Hers was shiny purple. Her companion's jacket
was shiny pink. Her son, well I had to presume, presume?
Presume he was. He was wearing little child clothes of some
sort. You didn't really look at his clothes. His head is so big
you don't remember what he was wearing.

When I was in grade three I was in a hospital room in
Lawrence with a boy younger than me. But the boy had a head
that was half the size of the rest of him. He had to lay it on a
pillow. That did not seem like a nice place to leave me. But I
thought it was interesting anyway.

But this kid didn't have a head that big. It was just like a
ten-year-old's head on a baby's body, let's say. Maybe not even
that bad.

I didn't know whether I would ever see him again. Them
again. I got as brave as I could and spoke to his mother when
her friend went to the ladies' room. This is what we said, more
or less:

"I hope you don't think I'm some sort of weirdo, staring
at your kid."

"I didn't notice you were."

"It's just that he looks exactly like me."

"Oh, really?"

"I mean exactly like I looked, what I looked like when I was his age, or I mean when he was ten or eight. When I was."

"He's a year and a half."

"Sure."

"Thursday."

"Anyway, he is a spitting image of me when I was eight in West Summerland."

"I don't see the resemblance at all."

"I wish I had a picture to show you."

Her friend was back from the ladies' room.

"Do you think Mikey looks like this guy?"

Her friend just giggled. She was a giggler, you could tell.

"I wish I had a picture to show you."

"Well, I never saw you a year and a half old so I don't think he looks that much like you. You're the second person this week to say my kid looks like them. Is this a new line for picking up young mothers?"

"Someone else? Did he look like me?"

"Not a bit. He had a long thin face, kind of pointed at both ends."

Her friend giggled.

The kid was staring at me with big calm eyes.

"How come he looks like that when he is only a year and half old?"

"Like what?"

I looked at her to see whether she was fooling me.

"He looks so old and wise. He looks like eight years old. He looks like an eight-year-old serious thinker boy."

"I sort of see what you mean."

Her son stared and stared at me. He could have been fifteen.

JUNE 22, 1988

No little me kid in Daphne's today. Just this talk that made me tired. Talk with the guy who walks in exaggerating how bad his back is aching. He sits down on the red banquette right next to me. I mean he has his little table and I have my little table, but we are sitting side by side on the long banquette. It is a banquette. That is what they call it. People fall off banquettes and later require steel pins in their ankles. I have heard that.

No little kids at all. But this geezer asks me whether I can see him.

"Nothing wrong with the light in here," I said.

"My wife can't see me," he said.

"I never get involved in other people's marital problems," I said.

"Not it," he said.

"I got my own problems," I said.

People talked this way to each other in Daphne's Lunch more than you might think.

"Oh sure, thanks," he said. "For nothing."

He always was a grousy old guy.

"I got this problem with a kid that's more than he ought to be," I volunteered.

Volunteered. How did I think of that word? I might as well admit that I have been having trouble thinking of words lately. Just now I remembered a word I wanted to use a while ago.

"Well, we all got our problems," the geezer said.

I just had to forget he was sitting beside me and go ahead and eat my grilled cheese sandwich when it came.

JUNE 23, 1988

The little me was there today.

We sat there looking at each other for a long time. A long time. I don't know, maybe an hour. Maybe less than that.

He wasn't wearing glasses but other than that we sure looked a lot alike. Like twins maybe.

I don't know what he was staring at me for. Maybe he stares at everybody. Maybe he was seeing what he will look like in fifty years. Or thirty years or whatever it is.

He looks to be about twenty years old I would say. Smart looking kid. Gets smarter looking all the time. Time.

In my dream last night a smart young Jewish professor says, "I do not use time to keep back space." I looked at his dark eye and tried to look like I knew what he was saying.

I don't even know what I was just writing. I do remember an amazing number of words, though, everything considered.

I figure I am still smarter than most people in Daphne's Lunch. Includes that little me fellow.

You want a battle of wits, kid?

Still, he's a nice looking boy. I do have to say that, don't I? Given that I'm talking about myself.

No, I'm not. This is a person in a greasy spoon. Somebody's kid. Some kid. I can't remember what I had to eat at Daphne's today. The usual, I would say. Daphne is never there any more.

I am. Both of me.

JUNE 24, 1988

cereal
hamburger meat
toilet paper
2% milk
vegs—brocc. or cauli.
60 w. light bulb
tea bags
toilet paper

JUNE 25, 1988

Twenty-fifth. Holiday of some sort, but not June.

Light was coming through the window like Mom used to be. Very bright light. Coming in like an angel.

Like a god. Coins spilling off him. Skirt made of golden daggers.

In the lunch place. I saw a kid in a stroller or sitting at a table, same thing. I mean you get something. Good to eat.

They were angry at me. Someone.

Wanted me out of there.

Later I noticed a dog staring at me. This was just around the corner. He wasn't trying to scare me. Just looking at me. I thought okay.

I didn't think okay. It was just okay.

Dog didn't look like anyone.

I never had that kind. Haven't got any dog now.

JUNE 27, 1988

dapne

he xtwo

eyen   like

mi yen

.   hee

. i i

gett msʃ   2 get

JUNE 29, 1988

PRETTY AS A PICTURE

Exactly how do you lie on your back in a canoe and look up at the sky and whatever is in it while the canoe drifts wherever it will, let's make it a lake rather than a river. The only time I have ever been in a canoe was on a lake, Trub Lake, as a matter of fact, where my brother lives now. He has an old canoe under a tree in his yard, but I've never seen him out on the lake. He's a golf guy, goes golfing just about every day, got an electric golf cart.

But how do you lie on your back, say, with your elbows up and your hands under the back of your head? Canoes have those seats in them, don't they, or are those rowboats? No, you kneel in a canoe. Maybe there's a strut or two going across from side to side. I guess that if you can manage the strut or struts, you could lie on your back. Carefully, till you got your balance, then relax.

Looking up, you can see a bird from time to time, maybe some overhanging tree branches, depending on how close you are to shore, if it's a lake, or the bank if it's a river. But I'd prefer a lake. If it's Trub Lake, and you are lucky, there'll be a little wispy cloud up there. This is all very relaxing, the sort of thing these city therapists tell you to imagine. Those tapes some people listen to when they're trying to get to sleep.

But I have been in a canoe just that once, and never flat on my back. I remember once listening to a funny argument about whether you could do it in a canoe. I figure anything's possible.

I wasn't in a canoe, of course, or she would never have been anywhere near me. I was lying flat on my back, all right, but I was in my own bed, the old brass bed my grandfather used to sleep in when I was a kid in the hills. My grandfather lived with us after my grandmother died. There were lots of sons and daughters in the family, but my father was the one everyone else knew was going to have my grandfather live with him. We had to build another extension on the house, and a special bathroom and all that.

The reason I was lying flat on my back was because I was feeling sick. This happens about two or three times a year. I get really sick and go to bed for two days, and then I'm all right, as long as I don't have to run or carry something heavy. I was in my first day of staying in bed.

She was in there to give me a kiss.

This made me nervous. It made me feel pretty good, of course, but it made me nervous, too. She is a good-looking woman, has a few freckles, knows how to make a wisecrack that isn't mean. That's a good reason to like a woman. But her husband and my wife were somewhere in the house.

My wife is pretty as a picture, and her husband is a tall handsome guy with a nose something like mine. But life is complicated. We all have our own points of view.

Actually, her husband should be telling this story, because that's what he does—he's a writer. I'm a painter, but I'm not very good. I make an okay living painting people who want to look important. I have a secret self, doing jacket illustrations for books. I've known her husband, or known about him, for about ten years. It's only recently that we've become acquainted.

I didn't say anything to her, but I was wondering, What if her husband saw her kissing me and took it the wrong way?

I would like to have remembered to take my trumpet out on the lake with me. I own a trumpet, have since I was nineteen years old, but all I can get out of it is the B-flat scale, and that when no one else is around. I like to imagine lying on my back in my canoe, playing that trumpet. Imagine what it would be like to be standing on the shore and hearing the trumpet, too, coming sweet and lonely off the rocky cliffs on both sides of the lake. Sweet and lonely I would never be able to manage, though. I wouldn't want to take my horn out on the water and blow the B-flat scale, that's for sure.

The west side and the east side of the lake are made up of those rocky cliffs, striped during the ice age. My brother's house is on the south side, in the middle of a row of houses. He stands on his lawn and drives older golf balls into the lake. There are a few little ledges on the cliffs, where brown grass and cactuses get a grip, and once in a while a tough little pine tree, old and knotty and small.

I'm trying to remember that day in bed now, and I think I might have been in there with the curtains drawn shut to fight off a hangover. We had a big party the afternoon and night before, and I acted like a bozo all night. This was probably because she was there with her husband, because they were going to stay in the spare room overnight. I suppose it matters somewhat, whether I was sick or hanging in with a hangover. My breath must have been something else.

But she came in and gave me a good morning kiss just the same. I don't think I would have had the nerve to do that if the situation had been the other way round.

I really liked getting kisses from that woman. I don't really remember what the first one felt like, but I remember she asked me if she could kiss me. I could have said no, I'll admit that. But what's the likelihood, especially if she meant just this once? I guess what I'm doing here is trying to get out of accepting any blame. What would you do? With those light freckles and greenish eyes. Come on.

I couldn't tell you the exact technical colour of those eyes. I haven't got a tube of it—nobody does—but I can mix it. A writer could only make a shot at it and maybe tell you what it made him feel like. If her husband, for instance, was telling about this day he might call the wall-to-wall carpet "beige" and use that as a kind of metaphor. It's more like ecru. Except in spots where I have carried a full cup of coffee.

You'll notice I haven't mentioned my wife much here. I know. That's one thing you can come down on me for. I won't deny that. She went to a lot of work for that party, too. We were supposed to become better friends with him and her. I really wish we had. I figure that's not so hard to understand, but I seem to be in a minority.

Well, what happened, then? I take it that if a person starts to tell you a story, something is supposed to happen. Things are supposed to lead up to things happening. I guess I'm more used to making pictures. What if a real writer, say, started in to tell a story, maybe like this one, and all he gave you was a picture or two?

I could paint a word picture—isn't that what they call it in friendly circles?—of the husband. I should say of *her* husband. Or of my wife. I have painted my wife a thousand times, but I would have a devil of a time trying to describe her. As for telling a story, you have already formed an opinion about my ability in that direction. I figure the real storyteller in the house could have been working on one right then. He could have been in bed with a hangover, but he wasn't in his own house, I guess.

There are interesting stories and not-so-interesting stories. Everyone knows that, and everyone has had to listen to both kinds.

I could make up a more interesting story, about how she went out of control and when she was bending over the bed to give me a good-morning kiss, seemed to lose her footing and tumbled into the bed, and we tore at each other's clothing, except that I was just wearing a T-shirt, and all at once the door slammed against the wall, and there was her tall husband, his face red and his hair wild. Or there was my wife. Pretty as a picture.

Really, all I wanted was for everyone to go away so I could spend the day deep in sleep, being rocked to sleep by the little waves. Lying on my back, looking at the branches hanging over the water, feeling the canoe rock a little but just a little from my smallest movements. I scratch my hip and the birchbark rocks a little from side to side. Birchbark. I don't know what it really was back then, or would have been, is more like it. Not fibreglass, I hope. Two of my friends have died of fibreglass. Wood of some sort, I guess, very light wood. But not birchbark, unless I was really lucky.

Sometimes I think I am one of the luckiest people that ever came down the pipe I came down, and other times, such as right now, I think I am fated to bad luck, to being deprived of those simple things that other people seem to take for granted. I think I haven't had my share of kisses in my lifetime, for instance.

Even those memories we make up during our leisurely hangovers can easily tip over into bad luck. I scratched my hip a little too hard, for instance, and capsized the canoe, dumped me right out on my face, and there I was, falling face down toward the bottom of Trub Lake. I found out just this year, though I had lived near Trub Lake for most of my childhood and boyhood, that Trub means Muddy. It was muddy, all right. Falling face down toward the bottom of Trub Lake, I had to close my eyes, the water was so murky. And it was cold. Cold water feels even worse when you're wearing a T-shirt.

And she was not trying to rip that T-shirt off. She only said good morning in her peculiar mock-mockery voice. I don't think she ever mocked me or anyone else, but she liked to make it sound as if she were mocking you. She said good morning in that voice, and in the tone of that voice you also became aware that she might have been saying "morning" for convention's sake. Then she leaned forward from the waist and gave me a kiss of very short duration.

I kept my mouth shut and hummed for one second. I would not let anyone experience my breath at a time like that.

Then with my eyes closed against headache and her departure, I heard the doorknob rattle.

Anyone could have been out there, outside that door she was closing. Well, I had a hangover, or else I was coming down with something, and all I wanted to do was rock myself to sleep. At that moment, if you asked me whether I would rather have a freckled woman giving me a little morning kiss or a gentle ride in a canoe on a muddy lake a long way from any human being, I would go for the canoe, fibreglass or not. Bright red. With my wife's name painted in white on the side of the bow.

CARTER FELL

Above the clouds he had eaten baked lasagne out of a rectangular white dish, and fixed in his ears, the plastic knobs offered the Pittsburgh Philharmonic playing Pachelbel's Kanon in D. If he was going to die in another fiery crash, thank goodness for this, serendipity. It was the name of a bookstore in Berkeley, and as it turned out, he did indeed make it there, following an alarming zoom of the new subway beneath, somewhere, the bay.

It was his first stay in San Francisco after thirteen years, a return he had put off by way of a distorted principle. For six years he had stayed out of Babylon altogether, but a year ago he'd gone swimming a few metres across the line, and that broke his private pact. Now, San Francisco, that is, North Beach, was another matter. It was the city where he had learned that art was not something you do, it is something that chooses every fault and virtue, after you volunteer to pass through its gate. The eye and the words are not tools as some had tried to teach him elsewhere, but a world you enter and mature in. Poetry here had killed its truest son.

But they had gone their way, diverging. Since his last visit, the city had been broken in two, not by the promised earthquake, but by the loud music and its victims, the kids with matted hair from the prairies, and magazine writers. San Francisco was no longer an artists' town but a journalists' temporary hot spot. Now they made police-car pictures for television here. For his part, he had gone east, to Ontario-Quebec, the country that had sporadically fed him its colonial dreams during his childhood. Now he lived in the western colony again, but this week he was returning north from his winter in Puerto Limón, and returning to the still standing site of his own civilization.

He dropped his suitcase and gadget bag in the room full of holes at the Swiss-American, killer across the hall grinning at him as he pulled the rickety door shut on its rattling lock, and hiked up to the bar on Greene Street. Fifteen years ago he had

been driven to the bar to sit and have a drink with their poet—
not an illuminating evening, but solid in his memory. The poet
was now dead twelve and a half years, but the bar was still
there, and so was he now, Spanish phrases falling off him like
dying insects. From the lovely cool swarm of San Francisco
midnight air, he walked into Franco's, and there he was, inside
a ramshackle American gay bar, the Christmas decorations left
up through late January attesting to the other defiance. A gay
bar, yes, but neither the one nor the other fabrication, not a
swishy aluminum piano lounge and not a waterfront leather
bar with tattoos flexed under every globe of light. Franco's is
the best bar in America. Grateful policemen drink there at
seven in the morning after a boring night's duty at the precinct.

As soon as he walked in he saw Carter's large being at the
only table, facing him. Carter did not recognize him and so he
had the joy of saying hello, Carter. San Francisco can be
depended on from the moment you arrive, a hundred rolls of
exposed film in your bag, a winter well spent. Pachelbel and
Franco's. At moments like this your life seemed worth living.

He put on a casual happy grin and said hi yah, buddy, and
Carter couldn't believe it. Then he bought Carter a Picon
Punch and there they were, the first time together at Franco's
who both loved this place.

Three months later he remembered this moment, a pen in
his hand now, and wished that all one's nights could be so
marvellous, and wished he could, after all that had happened
since, recall it all with more vividness, such as one could recall
the things outside oneself and time.

Carter the sculptor had been the master poet's lover some years before he had died, age thirty-nine, attached to hoses in a California hospital. Ted the poet, who had always seemed so large, was really so small beneath Carter the giant, a hale junkie then, it was all a story, and he knew it of the telling. Here now was Carter, dying so the story went in Vancouver, a precious new citizenship that can protect you against many threats but not against your past. How that counts the revolutions and adds year by year, organ by organ inside your body. Mine too, he thought, from time to time.

What are you doing here, asked Carter, sitting noticeably still as he always had.

Having a drink. I just dropped my stuff in Murder Hotel and ran right up, he said happily.

Carter just looked at him out of the eyes of a large body with no time for impatience. So he continued.

A couple of hours ago I was standing in a line in Lost Angeles. Before that I was getting sunstroke in the bottom left corner of the Caribbean. Surprised to see me, aren't you?

Carter broke into his lovely campy chirp.

You bet your life I'm surprised to see you. Aren't you surprised to see me?

Yes, but happy, too. I think that if I can expect to find anyone I know in Ted's bar it should be you. It certainly shouldn't be anyone else I know in Vancouver. Did I ever tell you that I first met Ted in this bar? He was sitting right about where that stool is. How come you're in San Francisco?

Chirp chirp chirp chirp chirp chirp chirp.

Wonderful, he thought. What a pleasant way to bring another lonesome trip to an end.

So Pearl didn't even blink. She gave me the charge plate and drove me straight to the airport. She's a wonderful woman.

You don't deserve her, Carter, he said.

We'll all give you anything under the circumstances, he was thinking. Though we will try to be rough about it, so that you won't be called upon to acknowledge our extra care. When it gets complicated like this, talk a little louder and express your minor feelings with heart.

I love this place. It seems as if I haven't left, I haven't been away for fifteen years, he adds, leaning back in his cane chair and looking at the titles on the jukebox. Surprised, he put in a quarter and played a couple of Frank Sinatra songs.

Boy, he said, shaking his head, and he and Carter smiled at one another.

*   *   *

The next morning he moved to the Sam Wong Hotel, and there he wrote away on his article, and then he went out for lunch. The very streets of the city gave him life, the life he had dreamed away under the snow of Canada. He recalled every bar, every hotel, every store, the kumquats in fact that he had pulled off the trees along the boulevard in Berkeley. In the afternoon he walked to Haight-Ashbury. The love-child, heavy-metal drug scene, the rock rainbow had come and gone during the time since he'd last been there. That was the reason he'd spent so long between visits. Who needs a San Francisco of teenaged Rabelaises? Now the city had settled back into its former life of unseen gangsters and alcoholic poets.

That evening he went back to Franco's. Carter didn't show up, so he spent the night sitting at the bar, watching the basketball game on TV. As soon as it was over, some gay fingers turned off the set, and it was time to look, just drink the inexpensive old-fashioneds, and trade quips and information with the bartender, Aldo.

He had last seen Carter at his birthday gathering in the little house overlooking the end of Burrard Inlet. Carter hadn't mentioned that it was his birthday, just invited through Pearl all the poets and artists and pub characters he knew, all the people who by description would "care for him." He had apparently spent the whole day cooking his marvellous unCanadian food, aromatic fowls in large pots, salads made of large greens and raw nuts, abalone with white sauce in shells, bread he had baked that morning. He stood in the doorway between the little living room and the larger kitchen, obviously unable to eat or uninterested in eating, a towering figure in a black robe, his face grey and thinning, his hair straight back as always, a large wine glass filled with vodka and grapefruit juice in high huge hand.

The record player in the other room played the soundtrack of *Close Encounters of the Third Kind* over and over.

How many times have you turned it over, Carter?

This is the sixth time.

Are we going to hear anything else? How about some Pachelbel, for instance?

There is no other music. The rest is all just this world, just dirt, just ashes. It has all been burned to ashes. The power exhaust of their ships incinerated all of it. We are left with all the music we need.

How many times have you seen that movie, Carter?

Eight times. Once on the giant screen in Seattle.

Boy!

They are here, you know, he said confidentially, a satisfied smile on the largely immobile grey face.

As usual when he heard Carter speak this way, he was shy, he turned away a little with a joke.

* * *

Once Carter was a savvy junkie lying with black horn players in Manhattan. He was a sculptor with a California kind of success. He knew the insider's view of the sex lives of the politicians. So when he said the UFOs were here and they were going to take us all to heaven, you thought he was grasping at straws, his brain cells were undergoing chemical change.

Twenty-five people were invited to the gathering. Nine showed up. Carter stood like a statue in the kitchen, a "greyhound" in his hand, his lips pursed. I'm forty-five years old, he said, in his usual half-whisper.

I didn't know it was your birthday. Congrats.

He smiled, his head so high. He was six foot four. He was up there listening to the saucers. Everyone knew he was dying, so sixteen people stayed away. After all that slow practical work, there was too much food, and it was delicious. There were halves of partridges piled on the warm stove.

People, the little group, began to eat. While they were eating, Carter disappeared. He had gone to lie down. Everyone talked, plates on their knees, as if they hadn't noticed. Soon they were ready to meet in other places, the beer parlour, the Arts Club bar.

Next night he went looking for Carter, who was staying with Dev, the poet who swept out Franco's. It took a while, the

North Beach streets running into triangles, but he found the number. He couldn't find the door, though. After a quarter-hour of foreigner's indecision, he looked up at the windows again, and there was Dev, visible through the dirty glass. He threw six American pennies, one after another, and at last one cent hit the window. Dev looked out and down at the dewy street, and waved, he would be right down.

They walked to the bar together, talking about Carter.

What is he doing down here? he asked, thinking that Dev would know he meant to say is he saying goodbye to his old mean streets.

Dev was not in a hurry to get to the bar, but he was steady in his path toward it. Besides being a poet he was a painter, not a California success, but a good painter, when he had the time and eyes to be one.

He came to see Michael Cause off. Michael is shipping for Japan and Formosa.

He walked a dozen steps.

Carter loves Michael, he continued.

So does Pearl. Michael spent six months at their place, I said. He couldn't keep his narrator in the third person any more, not through all this emotion.

Everyone loves everyone, said Dev, and he knocked a long thin American cigarette into his mouth.

When I was last here everyone was very busy hating everyone. The poets and painters and boy longshoremen were all fucking each other's lovers and saying terrible things about each other at dinner parties.

Yes, that's true. Don't you understand us? asked Dev. Once in a while, last fall in Vancouver, and now here, he made me realize I was about five years younger, and a Canadian.

I could never get them into group photographs, I said, lightening up.

The only group pictures you see from those days are of the New York poets in town for a literary uprising, said Dev, holding his cigarette like a suicide pill, and we were at the bar.

*   *   *

A few months later Pearl told me that in New York he was always getting lost, and usually finding himself in a bar. Usually at a table near the jukebox. Once they were all going to the beach, Pearl and Carter and the boys, deflated beach balls, plastic sand buckets, towels, all crammed into the hot subway, ready for a Sunday afternoon at Coney Island. She knew better long before they got there, but she gave up, and the family got out at 125th Street. Carter went for one at an African saloon, and the three blond-headed mortals went across the tracks for the long ride south. Carter came home next day, with sand in his shoes. A sort of cheeky magic.

*   *   *

That night I walked Carter home from the bar. I was pleased for some reason that he was wearing his old San Francisco outfit, jeans and denim jacket, black shirt, work boots. Like

Ted, but bigger. Carter was one of the few men I knew who was taller than I was, and heavier. And gay. He was, surprisingly, street drunk when we got outside, and I kept within a foot or two of him, prepared to steady him on the steep sidewalks.

When is he supposed to die? I was thinking. I had been told before going to Central America, but so much had happened to dismiss the winter.

Now it had been over a decade, but I thought I could find our way around these Italo streets to Dev's place all right. There was no one else on the sidewalks in front of the restaurants and whatever else was there at two in the morning. The St. Francis or somebody church stood in a California night across Washington Square.

I'm staying just across the square and up a block, said Carter, as we stood on the corner. A taxi prowled by, an advertising board on its rear. No, you aren't, I said, I was there several hours ago or at least last night, and it isn't across the square, it is in here a block and up a half a block, I think. I shouldn't have said I think. But I got him turned around. Now I'm straightened away, he said, it's up the top of this hill. I don't think so, I said, but I walked up with him anyway. It wasn't there. We stopped for a while as his body fought for breath. His throat was wheezing and I felt a sudden responsibility here a thousand miles from his house in North Vancouver.

Then his great work boots slid across the sidewalk and he fell to the concrete.

He was a heavy man. His devil had wasted away much of his flesh, but it was all I could do to lift his heavy skeleton to his feet. I had my arms around him and he had one arm around me, and I felt all of the human doom of his art then, art and its themes born out of the eternity we were so close to, I had a hold on love and death. In that silly collapse he had wet himself. I loved him, and felt more security than alarm. I felt as if I could now aim him for rest, and walk straight to Dev's place. I did, and I waited fifteen minutes while Carter climbed the stairs inside. I saw him in the unlit window and then I walked straight back to my hotel.

*   *   *

I had agreed to fly back to Vancouver the next day with Carter. At 8:30 I was out of the Sam Wong Hotel with my suitcase and gadget bag. The coast air was cold and the streets were shiny wet. A transvestite in silver high heels snubbed me when I said good morning. San Francisco is a comfy place in the early morning.

At Franco's there were several cops in nylon jackets and suntans, drinking brandy or whisky to wind down from their shifts. I didn't risk saying good morning, except to Carter and Dev. Dev was a mess—he had been there all night, washing the floor and catching an hour's sleep on the cot in the basement. Carter was wearing his lively red-plaid woolen jacket, good for the earlier morning, and ready for the north. He was drinking a lot of Picon Punches for his last day in San Francisco. I bought a long cigar and read the paper. Franco's is a nice bar in the morning. Fielding Dawson would not feel out of place but he wouldn't altogether like it.

Going home today, Carter? asked Angelo, who was wiping the bar.

He *is* home, I thought he would say, or I thought I would have him say that.

Yes, said Carter. Going home.

Will you be seeing that faggot poet?

I'll be seeing about twenty faggot poets, said Carter, in the high amused voice he used for banter and gossip. I loved him when he did his catty queen voice, which was one step along the way.

I mean the extraordinary one who published Ted's late great po-ems in his typical North Beach dear-me magazine.

You mean John the Arranger?

Yes, that's the one. Will you give him a message from me?

Sure.

Tell him to go fuck himself, said Angelo.

Now, I can't do that. We aren't good friends any more.

I looked up from the exciting basketball story in the *Examiner*. Vancouver is just the way San Francisco used to be, I said.

That's not true, not entirely true, said Dev. A lot of the people are dead. And the new blood that replaces them drink beer in loud barns filled with little round tables.

That made me nervous. I went back to my newspaper, and then I had a look at Carter. He was just ordering another.

We better go pretty soon, I said. I didn't want to have an uncontrollable event on the airplane.

* * *

Don't you understand us?

* * *

At the airport I paid the taxi driver, and then I did everything. Carter would have led us off to Zambian Airlines. The little bar was packed, and so once the bags were cleared away we went to the snack stand and I made Carter eat a cruller and drink some tea. His fingers on the dough did not shake, and they were not wasted. A sculptor's hands are twice as strong as any of his interior organs. Michelangelo's hands are still firm around a rosary in his tomb.

On the jet I ordered a Bloody Mary and Carter had a lemonade with little ice cubes in a plastic vessel. I didn't say anything but I supposed that he was straightening up, assuming an order pertinent to him and Pearl and the physician. But at the last moment before we started our descent into grey-green Vancouver, he had a double vodka while I drank a cup of coffee.

God, it is a job I would not like, being him, I thought. I thought of taking out my camera and fixing him then, and now, but I only thought about it.

Helen picked us up, and then we drove him to the university, where Pearl would be off work in an hour.

He was standing in the gateway of the Japanese garden as we turned to drive home. He was wearing a red-plaid jacket and holding a small blue bag. It was the last time I saw him.

Two weeks later I was in Toronto, talking with some Toronto people who knew how to look at photographs and words and turn them into a book. They too were from the West but now they were in Toronto, and every word they said and every movement their bodies made said this is the way we do things in Toronto. They led one to believe for a while that in Toronto they really did know how to do things we on the west coast are too innocent and too nice to have learned. So that sculptor in Toronto, for instance, would not share his energy equally between shaping mud and speaking love to a poet in ill health. Everyone like me needs a little Toronto and quite a lot of time forgetting Toronto. If Carter had ever taken a plane to Toronto he would have vanished like a drop of water on a hot pan.

In the evening in Toronto I ate part of a pot roast in the dining room of an old friend from the coast, and then I phoned Vancouver to find out how Helen was doing. She told me that Carter had died the day before. He had gone to bed in the middle of the afternoon and an hour later he had just died because he could not breathe.

Sometime last winter he was working on a series of small heads of his friends. I have seen the sketches he made for mine. It was as if he wanted to be sure we would all remain. I don't know why some things are important in a story.

*   *   *

Relationships very often go in this order: strangers, friends, distance, sickness, death, and funeral. Distance is very important. In a story readers look for distance.

I flew back in time for Carter's service, a week later. It was held on a cold afternoon in Pearl's backyard. We all sat on stools or blankets on the deep grass, poets and artists, homosexual friends, babies, some college professors, sons and daughters. Some were people I knew. Some were from New York or San Francisco, while others were the semi-permanent semi-strangers we often saw at Carter's parties. There were four times as many people here as there had been at Carter's birthday party. His scratchy-haired dog went from group to group, sitting at someone's feet for a while, then moving on.

I was cold, and that kept me from gathering all my feelings for the importance of the occasion. People were talking without the nervous conviviality of indoor funerals. Pearl and her sons handed around the blue mimeographed program. It was entitled "A Mass to Celebrate the Death and Resurrection of Carter McCammon."

*   *   *

Once, a year ago, Carter led me downstairs, into his basement. Past the usual pickle jars and washtubs, he led me to his damp place of solitude. He parted the curtain made of wooden beads, and I saw a wide bed on the invisible concrete floor; it was covered with a spread of cheap Indian design and strewn with Oriental cushions. Around it were some red and brown drapes. Against the wall stood a rude wooden table covered with photographs and papers, strange objects, hollowed herons' eggs, carved African animals, something tubular that looked as if it could have been old human skin, a lot of things I can't remember, a plastic bag of marijuana, sheet music, and so on. On the wall above the table was a large Canadian flag, not the Pearson maple leaf, but the Red Ensign from my childhood. I never did understand how I felt about that.

From the table Carter picked a small green-covered child's notebook. He opened it to the middle pages and handed it to me.

Do you recognize this? he asked.

It was one of the finest of Ted's poems, inscribed by the awkward hand I had seen only once before, fifteen years ago, and in fountain-pen ink. It was a poem we all loved. We knew that Ted was a great poet then, though his cult was only now making its effect known in the eastern parts of the continent. We loved him, and I do not know whether to say it is partly because he has been dead for thirteen years or because we simply do not think of him as dead.

Ted had died in San Francisco a week after I had left the city for Latin America.

He wrote that one afternoon while I lay on the couch across
the room, listening to some strange music, said Carter.

I didn't know what to say. It was inconceivable, though I
knew better, that the homely words written on this vulnerable
little notebook's paper, and read by this man in this dark
chamber just last night, are left by a person clear out of this
world. Ted used to say that his poems were recited by voices
from another star.

Carter was nicely preparing everyone, and it embarrassed me.

                        *   *   *

Polymorphous as our group was, it was a real mass we cele-
brated. Among Carter's people was a poet whose brother is a
young priest, and now they were both on the high back porch,
both in black-rimmed eyeglasses and straight-legged blue
jeans, Michael singing the Latin in a high beautiful voice,
Matthew handing him things. The Protestants and pagans on
the lawn sat with coats around their shoulders and sang along
in response as Michael had instructed them. I gave up trying to
feel a solemnity, and looked at my friends up there, and now I
knew what I was feeling was love, a human living with a great
deal of confidence fallen away. Michael did for us all, and
Carter, and Pearl especially, the grace that his blue jeans
suggested, of carrying on an authentic west coast Catholic
ceremony without condescension and without hipster sophistication. I had seldom felt more love for people in a group. Pearl
sat up front with friends, no tears on her face. Helen beside me,

who had no great patience for these people in the general
course of things, was moved to a serene quietude, and I knew
that she, who wore sweaters in May, felt more cold than I did.

In a rectangular pewter box, carved on all four sides and the
top with Oriental equine figures, was Carter's residue.

The sky, framed by the bare apple trees and mountain ash
of the sloping yard, descended from blue to a darker blue.

Four months later I am remembering that moment, a pen in
my hand, and accustomed to the fact that not all evenings can
be that marvellous, but wishing I could, accepting all that had
happened since, redraw it all with vividness, such as one can a
place, a house. I did not then have my cameras with me, and
though it was suggested to me that I might photograph the
afternoon and later the night in the crowded little house, I did
not want to.

* * *

I'd wondered whether I should tell Pearl about Carter's falling
down on the street in Little Italy. I decided not to, but how
many times did he fall noisily in that little house? We never
heard about it. For the first time now I am seeing a picture
of their tall sons grasping him under each arm and lifting
him again to his feet. For a second then I also imagined him
looking down at me writing this. At my father's funeral I held
my sister's hand in one of mine and my mother's hand in the
other, and wept. Then sitting there in the second pew behind
the empty first pew, I heard my father's voice.

It's all right, he said.

Now I wonder whether Carter knows that those people from elsewhere came to contact us. Either he knows or he doesn't. For sure I don't know. Between the two of us he has at best one chance in four of knowing. Though from his point of view, if any, he might see it as a much greater chance than that. When he was talking about those people coming here, when he was using his high-pitched gleeful voice about that, was he just preparing us some more? I was so embarrassed by his sincerity I just made a little joke about it and changed the subject; it was too close to what I was thinking.

It was getting colder, but on the blue paper everyone could see that the service would soon be over and the wake inside would warm people up. Michael came down from the high wooden porch and passed among us, offering communion, and everyone there took it. The bread had been made by Pearl, from Carter's recipe, and the wine they had made together that winter. We have to use it all, said Matthew, and so we did, and I saw Pearl give some bread to Carter's frisky little dog.

After that, Carter's older son, Brice, played his Spanish guitar, and sang a song he had written during the previous year. The words were all about the spirit and the spirit's longing for illumination, very spacey. Brice picked high notes from the strings for a long time between choruses. I did not like the words, so I lay on the grass to ease my sore back, and listened all alone. It was not as cold as I'd expected, and I lay still so that Helen would not think I was being dramatic. I was looking up through the bare branches of an apple tree, and as I listened to the clear music my eyes settled down too, and I looked as I always wished I would look at no other possible angles. Some of the limbs were closer and some were higher. I let my eyes fall on the bottom branches, and then rise one by one to the certain smallest twig at the highest breach.

I knew it had a corniness to it. But that too was stripped away, and I felt no embarrassment at all, for the first time in Carter's friendship and death. The sky beyond the tree was not yet black. It was a deep blue people mistake for black.

Once I lowered my eyes and looked at Brice on the porch. He was holding his guitar high, on a perfect 45-degree angle. There was only an inch or two of room, a few centimetres of room on either side of him, and then a candle burning near each arm. Also on the rail in front of him I remember seeing a pedestalled tray containing the host and two flagons of deep red wine, and so I know I have told the order of events wrongly. Draped against the wall below the rail was the large Red Ensign.

Then, sometime then, it was Pearl's turn, for the program listed "The Death Poems of Carter McCammon." The poems were, then, made by the two of them over a period of a week and a half. Pearl wrote them, and Carter lived them through, till the last. I have been planning to get drafts from Pearl and copy parts of them here, but now I don't want to. They will, in any case, be published on Earth within the next year. They are very hard to endure and we were fortunate to be prepared that evening. She spoke them clearly, and loud enough to be heard by everyone in that cold yard. They bared her completely, her anger, her disgust, her patience, and her god-awful love.

When she came to the words, I carry your few ounces home on my lap, and the lightness of your arm making stone of your life the last time, I looked for no reason to my left and saw that all at once between two telephone lines a planet appeared, a large white disc in a sky it made finally black.

The morning star.

Then we were praying together. Michael and his brother spoke the final Latin, and we picked up stools and folded blankets, and we all went up the stairs of the porch.

As usual in Carter's house there was plenty to drink, the food was excellent and there was a lot of it.

Rhode Island Red

Trust me, this will take only a fraction of the time it would take to write and read a novel, but there will be order somewhere here, faint order, human traces anyway.

If you were not in the South Okanagan Valley in the fifties, you will not be able to picture the scene I am picturing. But you can say this on the other hand, that no matter how well we think we are remembering scenes of thirty years ago, say, whenever we are given the opportunity to check those memories, we are invariably wrong, sometimes a long way off.

So I will have to do a little description, I guess, at least to get this going. The consolation will be that we will no longer have to listen to the voice delivering the goods in sentences that start with the first person singular pronoun. I like pronouns, but that one is not my favourite. Description, then. But be aware, won't you, that description will not bring you the authentic look or feel of the place, either.

We are three miles, because they still used miles then, south of the village of Lawrence. Lawrence could have been called a town, but the people who lived there persisted in calling it a village because it was cheaper when it came to taxes. No one could tell you how that worked, but everyone seemed to think that it made good sense.

Three miles south of Lawrence, let us say, in November. The orchards are just beginning to turn skeletal, the season's fruit picking finished weeks ago. Just across Highway 97 there is a funny looking apple tree. It owns perhaps only seven dry curled brown leaves, but there are apples hanging all over it. These are overripe apples, brown and wrinkled. If the orchardist working on his tractor up by the house were to drive down here and bump the tree's trunk with the front of his machine, he would find himself in a rain of apples that were useless except to the health of the soil covered right now with slick leaves.

He would probably also notice the chicken hurling its head at the pebbly ground beside the blacktop, and carry it under his arm back up the dirt road to the home yard.

There is no fence between this orchard and the highway. Fences are only a nuisance around the kind of farm on which workers are always moving ladders or trailers covered with props or empty boxes. As every orchardist along the road has said at least once, you don't need a fence to keep apple trees in, and any fruit thieves that come in uninvited at night are going to have to get used to rock salt in the ass. The kids around Lawrence figured that every orchardist had a shotgun loaded with rock salt or worse standing by the back porch door with the baseball bats.

Most families had chickens in their yards in those days. Even in town, where people would make little chicken runs out of chicken wire with a roof of chicken wire to keep large dogs out or to keep chickens in. It seemed normal to the narrator of this story, for instance, to keep chickens in the yard. When he was a kid in the South Okanagan in the forties, he had to feed the family chickens. That was enjoyable, whether throwing grain on the ground for those flailing heads or dumping the slop and watching them spear the corn cobs.

This chicken was a Rhode Island Red, a general-purpose breed created in the United States of America. It had a rectangular body and brown feathers of the shade called by parents red. By descent it had come from distant forebears in the jungles of Malaya. There were no roads through the jungles of Malaya in those days.

One time the narrator of this story planted some of the wheat that he normally would have fed as grain to his family's own Rhode Island Reds, and it grew. When the wheat plants were about three feet in height his younger sister pulled them out of the ground and threw them into the chicken coop. He still wonders today what made his sister think of doing that. The orchard in which their house stood contained lots of long grass, so she must have understood something about "wheat" when she ripped up his experiment to feed it to the chickens. Something about language. If he were to ask her now, she would just treat it as an old family joke. Why did the sister pull the wheat?

These families in the South Okanagan kept chickens for eggs and for chicken meat. That is why the Rhode Island Red was so popular. It produced lots of meat, and brown eggs, thought by superstitious rurals to be superior to white eggs in the matter of nutrition. White eggs were for city folks who also betrayed their personal biology with white sugar and white bread.

The male sperm lives in the hen's oviduct for two to three weeks. Yolks originate in the ovary and grow to four centimetres in diameter, after which they are released into the oviduct, where the sperm is waiting. Whenever we found a red dot in an egg we said, "Aha!" In the oviduct the egg also picks up the thick white and some shell membrane. Then it heads for the uterus where the thin white and the hard shell are added. The making of an egg takes twenty-four hours. Orchard mums are proud of hens that lay an egg every day. They are amused by the biddies that hide them in the yard instead of leaving them in the coop.

Now this one Rhode Island Red pecking away at pebbles and organisms at the edge of Highway 97. We certainly, I would think, cannot call her (or him if it is a capon) a central character in this little fiction. A figure at the middle of things, perhaps, but not a central character. A chicken does not have character. Unless you want to ascribe character to this Red's pecking and wandering away from the rest of the birds around the house, all the way down the dirt road to this shallow ditch beside Highway 97.

It is nowadays simply Highway 97, and not too much different from its condition in the late fifties. But in those days it was both Highway 97 and Highway 3, the alternative Trans-Canada. The two numbers, adding up as they did, really satisfied a teenaged boy who lived in and around Lawrence, but he does not appear in this story. There is a human being, you will remember, sitting on a tractor, doing something of value up near the yellow stucco house, where the rest of the Rhode Island Reds and the bantams were. His name is Kenn Oldfield.

If this fowl by the highway were a central character, as it might have been were the story a fable, it would have to be set down in a significant setting for the unrolling of the narrative. No, one supposes that fables do not have characters, but only fictions. Though Aesop's fables, for instance, are told in an attempt to mould character in their listeners, one can hardly ascribe character to, say, a grape-eating fox. If one were supposed to think about him in terms of character, a child might ask, Why does this fox desire to eat grapes, especially grapes that are out of reach?

In any case, even though we refuse character to the young hen in this instance, we can say a few things about the nature of the setting she had pecked her way into. The most salient because unusual feature, as far as she was concerned, was the highway. It was a normal western asphalt or tar macadam road, what is called in the trade a flexible surface. Gravel of fairly consistent size is covered with hot bituminous material that penetrates the spaces between the little stones and then cools and hardens. If you are a quick driver, you can just see a ribbon, as they say, of grey, or if it is the first month of a new highway, a ribbon of black. If your local member of the legislature is in the government's cabinet, you will see more black than do people in other places. If you are a kid walking along the highway, you can see the stones in the mix, and you have always wondered how many of them were Indian arrow heads. If you are a chicken pecking seeds and gizzard gravel into your interior, you will never get a pebble out of that hardly flexible surface.

There was a quick driver a few miles south, just passing Dead Man's Lake, heading north, probably going to the Co-op Packing House in Lawrence.

He was driving a truck cab in front of a big empty trailer that was equipped with a refrigeration unit, which could be seen from outside, a big square item on the top of the front of the trailer. The doors were open on the trailer, so one knew that the refrigeration was turned off right now. If the truck went by you slowly enough and you were on one side of the road, you would be able to see the other side of the road for part of a second right through the trailer. At the Co-op there would be some men and lads in cold storage ready to load the trailer of the truck with boxes of Spartan apples. Then the refrigeration would be turned on, and the truck would head to a large city grocery store chain whose name could be understood by anyone who could read now that the doors on the trailer were slid shut.

This truck was proceeding northward at about fifty miles an hour, which was the speed limit at that time as long as the road was straight, which was not often the case. Its driver was an old army veteran named Stiffy. He lived in the city where the grocery store chain was located, but he spent a majority of his days in the cab of his truck, trying to catch small town radio stations on his radio, stopping at roadside cafes where other rigs were stilled. He had had a conversation at Rhoda's Truck Stop in Castlegar this morning.

"Stiffy. How's it hanging, you old bugger?"

"Can't complain, Buddy. Can't complain."

The other driver's name was not Buddy. Stiffy called him Buddy because he couldn't remember his name, if he had ever known it. He called most men Buddy.

"I think I'm getting too old for this line of work," said the man.

"Know what you mean."

"No future in it either."

"Gettin' to be near time to pack it in and take it easy. Find out what my old lady does all day."

"Wouldn't know what to do with myself."

"Hah, I know what you do with yourself six or eight times a day, you old bugger."

"No, really. Guy owns the old bowling alley in Coleman. Been thinking of moving there, buy him out, live off the fat of the land."

"Oh, yeah, bowling is getting more popular every day they say."

"You know anyone goes bowling?"

"You know anyone wants to buy a Kenworth, one-quarter paid for?"

That was the conversation at Rhoda's, or most of it. During all that talk the driver we are interested in, if that is not an overstatement, was spooning up some chicken soup and biting at a grilled cheese sandwich. He often ate those things at Rhoda's, and something very much like that at the Orchard Cafe in Lawrence.

Now he was about ten miles south of Lawrence, braking behind a farmer in a rusty pickup truck halfway down Graveyard Hill.

In the high insect season trucks like that, and other traffic as well, brought about the demise of countless insects, fruit flies, grasshoppers, the black and yellow caterpillars that travelled the highway in huge groups. It was not high insect season now, but there were still some grasshoppers, those fleecy ones with wings that allowed them to fly in awkward trajectories. Despite the wings, there were some dead grasshoppers on the macadam, perhaps a head squashed flat but a thorax still complete. The chicken in question was out on Highway 97 looking for body parts of grasshoppers.

There is a well-known benefit to this kind of diet. If you get your eggs from some large city grocery store chain, you are likely to find, on opening them, that the yolks are pale yellow. If you boil them before eating them, you probably notice that the shells crack in the hot water. Those are eggs produced by chickens who are kept all their lives in the company of other chickens in small cages over conveyor belts. If you have your own chickens, and if they are allowed to forage, to eat bits of garbage and insects, their eggs will have tough shells and dark yellow or even orange yolks. They will taste a lot better than the grocery chain eggs. It won't matter whether they are white or brown; they will be higher in nutrition than those city eggs.

Stiffy's truck was no longer stuck behind the farmer's pickup. The farmer had become nervous about the sheer metallic weight behind him and pulled off the road, without signalling. Now there was a 1949 Pontiac sedan behind Stiffy's tractor-trailer. Inside the Pontiac were four members of the Koenig family, Mr. Koenig, with his sunburned face and gas station hat, and three of his teenaged children. The children were not in school because Mr. Koenig was taking them into Lawrence to get their shots. At the beginning of the school year in September there had been a nurse at the school giving out shots, but the Koenig teenagers had not been in school. They had been picking apples as fast as they could till it got dark in their father's orchard. Now there was not an apple at the Koenig orchard except for the boxes of Spartans in the Koenig basement. Eighteen boxes of Spartans and one box of Romes.

The Koenig kids did not care if they missed their shots. But there was a family in the orchard next to the Koenigs who had a son in an iron lung at the coast. Mr Koenig hated to think about him.

Two of the Koenig kids were in the back seat. One, the oldest and strongest, was in the front seat beside his father. His face was not as red as his father's. He had been born in this valley.

This is the sort of thing the Koenig teenagers were saying: "Murray told me the needle is yay long."

"Oh sure, did he tell you it's square?"

"What the hell do you know? When the doc says roll up your left sleeve, you always have to get some help from me."

"Listen, if you weren't a girl, I'd bash your teeth in."

"Just try it, jerk."

"Knock it off," said Mr. Koenig.

The road was never straight for longer than a few hundred feet. It looked as if they were going to have to follow the big truck all the way into Lawrence. Maybe they could pass him around the Acre Lots, but by then they were just as good as in town anyway.

Trust me, we are nearly there, and you will admit, I think, that there is some kind of order here. Human traces and some poultry thrown in. That's a bad choice of verb. Let's say some poultry added.

The poultry in question was now two-thirds of the way across Highway 97, trying unsuccessfully to back up and scratch at the surface, but finding better luck with its plunging head. There had not been any traffic for five minutes. That was unusual for that part of Highway 97, even in the fifties. People near the road could not help noticing when that happened from time to time, a feeling of peculiarity, as if the location were being *prepared* for something. Now that the tractor was just sitting up there beside the house, you could hear the telephone wires singing above your head.

Then Stiffy's truck appeared both to ear and eye. Its tires played a high note that would not descend. Stiffy saw the Rhode Island Red, saw it lift its head and fall momentarily on its tail as it turned to run back to its home side of the macadam, saw it disappear under the front of his machine. He did not see what a witness, had there been one, might have seen. The blur of red-brown feathers emerged behind the truck's long trailer, the living chicken picked up by the wake of hot wind and thrown high in an awkward arc into the air. It did not sail nor did it soar. It was a rectangular bird in the low sky, not flying but certainly falling now, and as it did, along came the Pontiac sedan. Mr. Koenig knew that it was a chicken. He even knew it was a Rhode Island Red. He had no idea how it had got where it was, hurtling toward the windshield of his car. He jigged the car slightly to the right, but the course of the hen was eccentric, and it became a smash of feathers and blood and claws and noise in front of his face where the glass became a white star. The car with four Koenigs in it was still moving to the right, and now the front right tire crunched into roadside gravel. Then the car went straight as the road went straight for a little while but in another direction. The Pontiac, having travelled for a moment at fifty miles an hour through long grass, stopped all at once against a leafless apple tree. If it had been the tree just to the left, the car would have been deluged with brown fermented apples.

All this made a noise. Stiffy, a half-mile north in the cab of his Kenworth, didn't hear any of it. But the orchardist and his wife did. It would not be long till they were both out of the house. Today they, like other people in the Lawrence vicinity, would be finding out what had happened. Tomorrow they would be thinking about why. Then they would talk about this event for a long time. Many of them would mention it in letters. As later events intervened, they would sometimes ask each other questions about this one.

THE ELEVATOR

Last night I was thinking: there I sit alone in the dark room with a little portable television —we face each other with the lights of our opposite eyes, lenses bending toward each other, and in the dark I suddenly know what it is coming in rays to my eyes, through them to my front brain—the blue light of the television, the open end of the set, it is actually a hole out of this darkness, through all walls into the open world. It is an extension of my eyes, the televison set and the invisible camera somewhere at the other end of the wires. I can sit in my darkened room and see into the world, whichever direction I'm looking at the time. Dip—look into my bedroom, young wife in silk to her knees, husband with tie hanging loose in front of him like an Anglican minister thing, talking to each other, and my ear is there too in their room, they are shouting at each other, and I see—my eye looks down at them from the ceiling and the walls have ears.

Till I thought, How still I'm sitting. Sure, so I can watch into the New York bedroom, zoom from airplane over the Riviera to look at bathing suits. No, because I'm necessary there. Can I remember turning the television on? What was I thinking at the time? Did I do it on purpose? I hesitate to think it. Am I annexed by the camera? Part of its action. The brain for its eye. Or worse. It came into the room to look across at me, then stayed there all the time while I came in and went out, it was waiting for me, always there when I came in with bottle of beer and newspaper, turning on the dial, to look over the top of the news. Come here, fingers.

"You. Television. Who needs you?"

"This is probably the salad oil you're using now."

"Up yours with your salad oil."

The cat jumped down off the wooden table where she'd been licking the dried food on yesterday's plate, and she made that throaty meow as her front feet hit the floor first, then her back ones, then gathered and sprang into a slow walk across the floor to me, tail in the air, her eyes now adding to the television, looking at me. What if television looked from a cat's eyes, in the dark? What's in that bedroom then?

The cat walked back and forth in front of me, rubbing her sides against my legs, stepping heavily with one cat foot on my toe. She was hungry. Welcome aboard. Neither of us had eaten since the day before. But for the cat it was sad. I hadn't let her out, and she'd shit in the empty bathtub again, and that was the last food she'd eaten, already hard and black in the white tub. Down the drain with you all—cat, shit, television. I got up and went out. The cat scooted out with me. As she disappeared around the corner of the house her tail went down, crouch already in the back.

"Good hunting, Janet."

Moreover thou hast taken thy sons and thy daughters whom thou hast borne unto me, and these hast thou sacrificed unto them to be devoured. Is this of thy whoredoms a small matter, that thou has slain my children, and delivered them to cause them to pass through the fire for them?

Ezekiel claimed that God said that to Jerusalem, but Zeke had been reading the older prophets, including several false ones, and he knew that's what the folks wanted him to say. They're still saying it, and Jerusalem among others is still doing it. I was one of the lucky children who hadn't passed through the fire. But I'd always taken precautions. Going down in an elevator, I always flexed my knees in case of a runaway crash. But I had lately got too involved with this too—thinking too hard about a burst blood vessel in the brain can cause a burst blood vessel in the brain. Then where are you?

Outside the house, looking at the snow.

Maybe a couple quarts of fuel in the gas tank, so I started it up in the dark and drove lights out through the streets, lighted by blue gaslights of Alberta natural gas, shining off the black steel of the car stretched out after the windshield in front of me, till I got downtown in the East End, Eighth Avenue, Sunday night, no stores open, wind in the dark flipping Saturday's paper end over end along the sidewalk till it came flat against dark red 1910 bricks. Cornices two stories higher jutted into the wind like leading edges of aircraft. I stopped the car and got out, thinking I was a professor, professional before I came to Calgary, so I have never walked alone in the East End purple wine part of town here as I had in Vancouver. And here there were no pigeons on the sidewalk.

The wind was cold, and at select corners it blew up peacock tails of snow, into the face turned the wrong way. I was the only one on the street. It was early March, no end to winter. In Vancouver the crocuses were popping up in people's lawns. I met an old man in a dark coat that came to his heels.

"Cold night," I said.

"You're right there," he said.

Without calling me sonny or young fellow. Here there's not much trouble about differing ages. The old men wear shoes with cracks down the back. The young wear boots that will eventually wear out. In the windows of the second-hand stores there are boots for eleven dollars, bright yellow next to bright yellow guitars and shiny flip-down toasters, and the big jack-knife with twenty blades in various degrees of open.

I watched the man walk farther along the sidewalk, his hand up on his bald head, walking carefully so the broken shoes wouldn't fall off his feet, and I noticed he was Chinese, the darkness rushing in to fill the place between us.

What is your name what is your name? Long coat frosted by the wind, moving into the loom of dark East Eighth Avenue, snow blowing into long skidded footprints, collar blown against my chin, something glanced off the side of my head and struck hard downward on my shoulder. I turned and crouched and it was dark there in front of me. I hit out and grabbed at movement, hands sliding in wet darkness as he moved away and came back. It was in his hand at the side. My one arm was numb, hanging useless, but I stepped that way and hit him low in the middle and he spun slightly to my side and I kicked out and missed. The street was gone, the town was gone, the old Chinese man. The thing came at me again, past my face, and I knew my only way was to rush, and I swept him, so he must have been small, against the brick wall, and hit him as fast as I could here out of the wind. I hit and held him against the wall with my body, a knee coming up against my thigh, looking for my soft groin. I saw the head for a second and smashed with my fist and back with the back of my hand, and it was hard, bones of my knuckles coming through skin. I felt his head give way, and it hit the side of the building. He fell into the pile of snow at the base of the wall and I kicked him, but he didn't move. The thing was still in his hand. I walked away, hurting, close to the wall, and toward the car. I hadn't seen his face. Old or young, I hadn't seen him. I bounced off the wall as I walked away.

In the car I sat with the engine running and fumbled with cigarettes till I got one in my mouth, the cigarette very little in my thick lips, the cold and the pain taking away all taste. I started the car and drove north, into the wind and snow.

"The temperature in Calgary a chilly three degrees," said the radio.

Chaucer. I've done Chaucer, Shakespeare, Donne, Milton, Blake. Now Pope, Wordsworth, Shelley, Browning. Professor.

People outside the university call me Professor. In a town like Calgary—city they like to call it but the railroad tracks still cut it in half, demonstrably, like the small towns that clamp around the tracks from east to west across the prairies. In February of this cold winter dead antelope lay frozen along a hundred miles of Alberta tracks, stiff legs pointed up at CPR passengers rolling by, eating turkey sandwiches with gravy in the dining cars. Calgary is eighty miles from the mountains and hundreds of miles from the nearest city, fed by television towers and the boxcars that carry newsprint. This university is now four years old, where teachers from Germany and Chicago and Vancouver speak to inmates of Calgary about far foreign things.

That's where I was going. I had left the apartment where there was no food, and the cafes downtown were closed. Couldn't stay there now, a body lying against the wall, dead or alive, probably alive, and young or old. Small, with something in his hand. The car drove me out to the old Banff highway, turn left at the university road, around to the bus stop.

Outside the wind was stronger here on the edge of the prairie, blowing in from the Rocky Mountain Trench snow, piled for days waiting for a wind. I kept my collar up and bent over, walking to the library. My office on the fourth floor. All the lights were on; a few students would be there on the coldest night.

"Sir, I've been doing some reading."

"Good."

"I've heard that Blake was crazy. How are we supposed to read his poetry? I mean—"

"As if he was crazy. Do you think Jesus was sane? Don't underestimate Jesus, either."

Jesus tipped against his own dark satanic windmills. The glass front of the library building loomed yellow in the dark wind, snow cutting around the straight corners, glass holding it off from the books. The hole in my right shoe allowed wetness that would dye the bottom of my foot the colour of whatever sock I was wearing. In the library no one needs shoes. Eyes.

The heavy glass door gave way to the wind half open, and I stepped into sudden heat and stillness, and the drifted snow started to melt at my throat. What time is it? Ten o'clock right on. Students—young girls with ski slacks and boys in red poplin jackets—were being rushed out of the building by skinny library women anxious to be home in time for the late show. I rode the elevator upstairs to the fourth floor, my office.

The lights were bright oblongs on the ceiling, this place meant for stacks of books, but now, temporarily they said, full of cubicles, offices, each with bookshelves, desk, chair on wheels, blackboard, pin board, piles of papers, ashtrays, and curious oblong wastepaper buckets emptied every night by unseen hands, large windows in a room full of easy chairs, lounge, with west windows, black now, mountains in the distance, snow hissing on the glass.

I was there to do something meaningful. I sat down and unfolded a lined paper and made marks on it with a red ball-point pen.

I opened a book and started to read a long poem by Robert Browning, but I stopped after a dozen lines—somebody in Renaissance Italy talking in long lines.

There were no footsteps in the hall. All the other offices were empty. Nobody getting ahead but me.

I smoked a cigarette and carelessly threw the burning end on the floor.

I continued marking papers in the silence that's the same anywhere there's an empty school—numbers nailed to the doors now with no meaning, blackboards within closed rooms, administering to rows of empty seats. Chalk dust could fill the air without liming any pink lungs, like the silence, in those rooms and halls so used to the fullness of talk. I make my living by being able to talk, me, so shy I couldn't raise my questioning hand in a classroom full of my peers, most of them stupid, afraid of getting a job. I was afraid of getting out of the wide halls and desk-filled rooms. The papers in front of my eyes on the grey-topped desk weren't familiar. I'd never written anything like that when I was a freshman—hesitant, awkwardly trying to fit long nouns from lecture notes into English sentences, with verbs, so shaky, so unsure. It made my heart soft as it always did. I wanted to sit close to each one, boy or girl, shadowy Walt Whitman teacher, and tell them not to try to make sense of the coincidence of bafflement in the school books of stone university, and the warm fluid that welled threateningly and buried between their soft bellies and seldom-touched thighs.

They could so obviously offer a kind of comfort to me, none of them terrified or bewildered by television; they could sit in partial observance and scrutinize the weekly trials of a blood-hand doctor, and sympathize with his patience for the sudden appearance of bottled salad oil. I was certainly gifted with speech—I could hold them, thirty at a time, and speak slowly as I wanted, authority coming from the verses in my own 170 pounds. But there were a hundred thousand television screens in Calgary, burning chill blue in dark March nights behind heavy window drapes. Could I hold up my end in a face-to-face encounter? I dropped my red pen on the paper and wheeled my chair back to the shelves of books.

There was dried blood on the knuckles of my right hand. Time to get up like the clean-conscious American on the screen, go out and, like they say, bathe the hand in warm water, then cold water, it closes the bloody pores. It feeds the bloody cat. I got up to leave, grabbing coat from the rack and carefully fingering the thing on the edge of the door, locker of offices, opener of minds, fair friends never met.

BERGEN, Norway (AP)—Norwegian pigs are becoming so idle they are biting each other's tails too much and causing a rise in infectious diseases, a slaughterhouse veterinary surgeon has reported.

FALSE TEETH—Chewing efficiency increased up to 35 percent.

New, new.

I walked then, head down, to the elevator, flexing my knees experimentally, slightly, while walking, my worn suede shoes phantom in the empty hall. Push button. Red arrow light. Distant down sounds of lurching machinery. When it came I walked in, looking at the shape of my toes through the suede. The door whispered shut behind me. Then the lights went out, and the elevator stopped going down. My knees flexed without my thinking of it. The liquid in the top of my head dropped abruptly to earlobe level. I composed myself, knowing there was a power failure, ready to wait. I'd seen it happen before; all bright yellow lights would be gone from the windows, and the eerie spotlights with power batteries would be shining down from the high walls, a selective light in the gloom of stone corridors. My fingers had curled into a fist, slightly opening the cuts again, dab of fresh blood. It was absolutely black in the elevator.

And breathing. A scent, perfume. She was in the black too, I hadn't known there was anyone else in the elevator, someone left after the doors were locked. That had happened before, too.

The breathing was right beside me, a hand touched my chin, end of fingers, she was walking slowly in the dark, hand out in front of her, it touched me for just a second, then was snatched away. I stood still. Her breathing was not back where it started from. I was breathing too, and maybe that would make her feel all right. Because I had no idea what she looked like, how old, how big, I had had my head down coming into the elevator.

"What happened?" she whispered. Her voice was very close. I wondered why.

"Power went off," I whispered back across close darkness. "It's okay. We just have to wait."

"Couldn't we yell or something?"

"Too late at night, nobody would hear us."

There was probably a janitor or a late-working librarian. Well, no sense complicating things. What good would yelling do? No amount of yelling turns on the lights. That had happened before, too. She must have moved quietly because I could feel her arm brush mine. It went away, and came back. I was comfort in the dark, I suppose, the professor. Meek and mild George Delsing puts on his magic necktie, mutters the ancient words of the scroll, and becomes: Professor-Man!

The dark man in the elevator put his arm out slowly, slowly, plunged up to the shoulder in the darkness, around probably behind her, and drew it toward him till it touched. Her. She was wearing a coat for the cold, here unnecessary for the dark, a man could be wearing nothing; teaching in a school for blind girls, walking naked around the room, in and out among the blind, dark alleys of the elevator. The girl, the woman, didn't move. Till I felt her hand on my wrist where I was holding her. I placed my other hand on her, and she came up to my neck, her hair scented under my chin. Then I felt her hands on me, here in the university, all over my body, timidly on the front of my pants, hesitating a moment on the broken skin of the knuckles.

Dew melon dew melon lying half-hidden under the broad green leaves. The earth is rich.

I began taking her clothes from her, began with her long coat, and it was easy there in the dark, no sight of awkward lifted elbows, it was as easy as taking the linen drape from a nude sculpture. Her blouse came undone and over her shoulders, and her hands were at her skirt so that it too came off, down, easily, fell to some dark corner of the elevator. A few clasps, a few caresses of my hand on her back, her leg. My fingers went inside her panties and gently pulled them down over the round buttocks. My clothes came off easily, her hair on my naked shoulders, and we eased each other down on the pile of clothes, breath in our faces, moisture in the vales of God's morning, and we fell to the deepest darkness, flowers cascading over the head of the young hero.

When my blood was moving fastest, the knuckles on my hand were hurting. Broken flesh had met broken flesh in the dark.

She whispered, "When the lights come on, I'll have my back to you, and you mustn't look at me."

"But who are you?" I asked. "I want to see you again—"

But I did as she bid. As the doors opened on the main floor, she spoke again.

"For all you'll know, I might be one of the people in your class."

I waited as she asked, ten minutes, till she would be completely away from the university. My body was warm, and this would last for a few minutes in the cold night outside. In two days I would meet my class again, and the eyes of all the girls in the class would be looking at me, and they would all be listening to my voice. Wordsworth.

When I got home I had a bag full of groceries, on credit, and among them was a can of cat food. If I had a dog instead, maybe it could have licked my aching knuckles.

JOINING THE LOST GENERATION

One Saturday night in early spring, at a busy corner of the Edgware Road, a pushcart with two policemen in attendance drew the curiosity of passing Londoners. On the pushcart, partly under a blanket, lay a twenty-year-old soldier of some sort, three-quarters asleep, a smear of blood in his hair.

One morning in April of 1915, just before his eighteenth birthday, he had been sitting in a library at the University of Toronto, trying to read the Roman poets. As to the weather, it was an April day out there, this morning's rain in the trees, hoofprints in the mud where the playing field ended. A young man in a scratchy-looking sweater vest approached his table. He was a librarian or an assistant.

"There is a telephone call for you, from a friend, he says."

He left his books on the table and took the call. Then he headed for the nearest recruitment station. When he came back to pick up his books, he was wearing an ill-fitting army uniform, puttees inexpertly wrapped. The literature student was now a member of the Toronto General and University of Toronto Base Hospital Unit.

He was going to carry stretchers in no man's land, rescuing gallant lads, dodging explosions and earning a Victoria Cross. There was a tattered Union Jack serving as a backdrop.

"Well, that one's 'ad a few too many, 'eeyaz," suggested one of the curious on the Edgware Road.

He could not know that he was looking at a future Nobel Prize winner and prime minister of one of the pink colonies. This was a chap who had never had a drink in his life. Or a cigarette. Or a roll in the hay.

Unlike a lot of young military gents who went to the city without permission of their base commander, he was not under the influence. He had just been bowled over by a London omnibus.

But first he had to get to the war. The week he spent in the hold of the troopship *Corinthian* was the worst week of his life. He had never smelled men before, or perhaps a sweaty shirt in a dressing room. There were horses with bags under their tails. It was dark. He contributed to the odour.

The summer at a camp near Dover was, by comparison, pleasant. Soon his outfit was in the Egyptian desert between Alexandria and El Alamein, waiting to make commendable sacrifices at Gallipoli. There might be Victoria Crosses at Gallipoli. At Gallipoli the Australians did the things that made them a conscious nation. But when the Toronto General went to a theatre of war it was to the mud of invaded Greece, in the old clouted country outside Salonika.

So much of this war was done in the dark. He had not been able to familiarize himself with any of the faces in the hold of the *Corinthian*. Now the enemy planes that made it past the barrage balloons were trying to drop bombs on the biggest city in the world, and it was so dark that no one saw the bomb drop out of the high darkness, only the bright flash of the detonation and the glimmer that remained afterward.

If you were lucky you saw the glimmer. There were all kinds of luck in this war. Some people were lucky to be alive. Some wished they had been lucky enough to die. Then there was the luck about finding a supply of whisky or gin. The soldier under the brown blanket did not drink spirits, though. He was an intelligent Protestant from Ontario.

In Greece he was not dodging bullets in no man's land. He was cleaning backsides and emptying bedpans in three hospital shacks where they brought infantrymen who were being chopped up by the Austrians and Bulgarians.

After a month he graduated to the operating room. But the first time he saw a knife lay open the innards of a naked soldier, he fainted dead away. The next day he was reassigned to the quartermaster's store. This was a dismal kind of Europe. In later years he would be the hero of the Swiss ice hockey team. Now he got a letter from his brother, who was posted in England. His brother called him "the Fighting Grocer." But he worked diligently at the quartermaster's store. Somewhere he had learned to do his best whatever the job. He was a really good Ontario Protestant, and that is enough said about that.

He would never have any memory of getting from the Edgware Road to the hospital. It would be in the dark, in the dark inside the dark because he was without consciousness, like the etherized boys he had seen in Macedonia. For six weeks he was just about a civilian, in a hospital and then a rest home. He was a Protestant, and this was the first time he had ever rested. And someone else saw to the bedpans. He lost his desire to go to France, either on foot or by plane, and he forgot his aim to rescue British democracy. From now on he would be a peace man.

While he was in that rest home a half-breed from the Thompson River country won a cross for capturing a German machine gun nest. The Canadians had hanged his father. When he got home he would be unemployed again. His grandfather had been shot by the Indians. There was no rest home in the Thompson River country.

The ocean had made him sick. Surgery had made him faint. What else could he not abide? He was from Ontario, and he was deathly afraid of heights. So in a spare moment in the store he applied for transfer to the air corps. One afternoon at the strip near Salonika, he snagged a ride in the front cockpit of a two-seater that lowered two wings and headed north, up beside Mount Olympus, higher than the gods, these little human monkeys, and over the Bulgarian lines. He was a little sick but he did not want to be a grocer any more.

All the boys wanted to be in the air corps. They dropped his application into a drawer that no one would ever remove anything from. He started wearing a white scarf anyway. He was the boy pilot of Salonika. He waited and waited. He could not even get a ride in a cockpit. Finally, he bent over his counter and wrote a letter to his father. His father was a Methodist preacher who read a lot of books, but he also knew Sam Hughes, the preposterous moustache who thought he ran the Canadian war effort. Somehow Sam found a string to pull, and in the spring of 1917, the preacher's son was in the infantry.

But he was not going to carry a malfunctioning rifle up a machine gun hillside in the mud of France. First he would be a second lieutenant at officer training school in Oxford. While his classmates covered themselves in beer at student pubs, he explored the colleges, memorizing the chapels and pacing the football fields. He was in a hurry to get to France, but he expected to return. He wanted to be on a team at Oxford. Once he was finished changing history, he wanted to teach it to young men from Ontario.

At the rest home he had discontinuous talks with a young man who could not face the dark. He was afraid to go to sleep in the dark, but when he stayed awake all night, he lived in fear that someone would turn out the last ward light. He saw the nurses' white shoes and these kept him alive, he said.

"You will get better if you sleep at night," he said.

"I know that, but I cannot sleep, Lieutenant," said the young man.

"You have not slept nights as long as I have been in here," he said.

"I should not have been in this war."

"This is not a good war for young men," he said.

The young man lit a cigarette, flinching a little when the flame popped.

"Do you think he is a young man for whom the war has been a bad idea?"

"Who?"

The young man gestured toward a body wrapped in cloth. His head was wrapped in cloth. Under the cloth, you just knew, just knew, he had no face. He could have no knowledge that he had been tried for treason and found guilty. But here he would have to stay and convalesce. He would convalesce without ever standing up again, without ever seeing anything again, without being able to think about.

Every day a woman came and brought fresh flowers for the little table beside his bed. Maybe he could smell them. Freesias.

"A very bad idea, this war," he told the young man.

At officer training school in Oxford, he had a captain, a hairy man, who had been sent home from France with battle fatigue. That was an option for officers in those hard months of the war. Some famous English poets and some men who would have gone on to become famous poets got killed one way or another in foreign mud. But this one managed the battle fatigue. He also called in a few upper-class favours and saved another officer poet from court martial and God knows what punishment. It was the great discovery these gentlemen were making, that once war got done with guns that can reach into the unseen, war is in all ways ignoble.

This captain would live to be ninety years old, and publish a lot of poems, and live away from England, and he would be remembered for a book about mythology, that and two poems that would feed the college anthologies for the rest of the century. One was a clever poem about his penis. The other said that composing poems can stave off the noise that brings on battle fatigue.

"We spell away the overhanging night," he wrote. "We spell away the soldiers and the fright."

The young Methodist from the University of Toronto must have seen doubt in the eyes of his captain there in Oxford, but he still looked forward to defending the Empire. Years later he would write, "Our views were not yet contaminated by revelations of pre-war political manoeuvring by the European governments in the pursuit of power rather than principle." He had to write prose like that. He was a successful politician.

Now when the flying corps asked for more pilots, it was not hard to figure out why. In this war the shortest life expectancy belonged to the flyers on both sides. Maybe this was the only place left for gallantry. Far above the filthy terrorized young men clinging to the ground below, the pilots could duel. They could empty belts of machine gun ammo at one another, or wave and dive out of range. The moviemakers were wild about the flying boys.

He volunteered again, and this time he was eagerly accepted. Despite all the corpses and amputations he had seen in Macedonia, he must have retained his thirst for patriotic glory. Well, it would be the worst future possible if the Huns were permitted to undo the work of the Empire. He wondered how the Huns could have built airships that worked as well as their own. Or maybe he just wanted to give in to his fatalism.

Years later he wrote to me, "You went on until you were killed, like all your friends were being killed. The only thing that would save you from being killed was being wounded, and getting out of it."

I wrote him back. "You sound like Ernest Hemingway," I told him.

"Hemingway lived on Spadina Avenue," he told me. "A few blocks from the university."

There was a lot of turnover, then, in the flying trade during 1917, and the training had to be done fast. His trainer allowed certain idiosyncrasies in the air. But he did not like his name.

"Lester is no good. It is not belligerent."

This man never had to meet his brothers, Marmaduke and Vaughan. The Methodist preacher was normal in a lot of ways, but not in the naming of sons. We never learned where these monikers came from.

"We'll call you Mike."

For a couple of weeks the new airman chewed Wrigley's Spearmint Gum to steady his nerves. He was too terrified to stand on the roof of the aerodrome, but sitting in the cockpit of a noisy smelly plane, he was too busy to faint. He entertained his trainer with high bouncing touchdowns. Mike was a creative aviator, dodging telephone wires, landing on the hypotenuse.

Then one foggy day Mike's teacher hopped out of the two-seater and sent him up solo. He was operating a Grahame-White, more commonly known among his fellow doomed as a box kite. It was a cloudy day. Well, it was England. Mike went into a bank for his bounce-down, and the kite just kept banking, and it crashed rather than landing. He walked away, as they say, from the inelegant plane.

They gave him a few days off. He had a scratch or two, and a couple of bruises, but these were not the reason for his confinement to the ground. It was a matter of form, something the British were very good at. Yes, you should get back up on your horse, but you should gather your wits and understand your determination. There were enemy to shoot down, and it would take a nice combination of recklessness and narrow purpose. You are, we remind you, confined to base.

But Canadians in England had a reputation to uphold. Canadian lads were rowdy and horny. On Saturday he caught a ride into London. Come on, any colonial boy would be drawn to the biggest city in the world. Piccadilly, eh? He met some friends, still living flyboys, and went out for a good time. For the Methodist preacher's son this meant having a good civilian meal, well, as good as you could find in England, and arguing about sports. The others were just what you might expect, but for him, no drinks, no cigarettes, no you-know-what.

"The Grahame-White," said an English pilot with no hair on his face, "is a marvelous target. They should paint the roundel much larger on the fuselage."

"If I could just keep that kite in the air, I would fly it to France tomorrow," said Mike.

"Our own gunners would bring you down, just because it is such a provocative sight, this unflyable airplane."

"They would wing you for amusement."

"Bring you down with a sporting piece."

Who knew how much time these young men had to make fun of their own mortality?

In what way is this a short story I am telling you? It is a little look into an important life. There is a baffling lack of literary principle here. Should I leave such interpositions out at this late date? Someone is going to be angry no matter what I do. Imagine—getting angry at the way a person tells a story.

You could always try to read the Roman poets.

Recently, I have to admit, a really good short-story writer I know sent me a new story by email, and I was so happy with the way it went along, never snagging. When the short story is mentioned, his name comes up. Mine doesn't.

When Lester's name is mentioned, they talk about peace, not about careless death in the First World War.

All at once the air-raid sirens commenced honking. In 1917 the air raids on London were nothing like those in a later war, but they were the first air raids that London had ever received. They were taken seriously. Mike went out into the unlit streets and boarded an unlit bus that would take him toward his base at Hendon. London was odd in the nearly complete darkness. It could have been Newtonbrook. When the day's light came, he would be in the sky over the Channel.

But when the driver heard a bomb explode a half-mile away, he stopped the bus right there on the Edgware Road and ordered everybody out. The lieutenant headed across the street and was clobbered by another unlit bus. There was no walking away from this wreckage.

In the First World War the doctors talked about "neurasthenia." At war the poets could get it and so could the history students. In the hospital they did not have any Romans for him to read, but there were a lot of stories. Around him were boys whose legs were under the ground somewhere in northern France. He did not tell his story of the omnibus unless someone asked him directly, and in this place the young men did not do that.

Someone told him that the young man without a face was also from Ontario. He was under arrest, someone said. Mike no longer heard imperial music. He did not imagine machine-gunning a German kite. He had to fight the embarrassment of the bus, but in a while that was all right. In the rest home one could look directly at a young man who sat every day in a white wicker chair beside the pond and looked at the water and never said a word. Someone said that when a letter came from New Zealand he could not recognize his wife's handwriting.

After six weeks of recuperation, he was taken to a ship that would carry him back to Canada. This time he would ride above, in the grey Atlantic light. He was leaving his brothers to fight the war in Europe, and he did not even know the fighting names their trainers had given them. One was in the trenches and the other in a navy plane. He did not expect to see them again.

Some short-story writers will try to make you see the room their hero is in. But imagine those shell-shocked amputees in that rest home. You can be sure that the stories they told one another were better than anything any writer would ever make up. And when they were home again, their families would notice that they never told any stories about the war.

Mike would one day become the most famous peace negotiator in the world. He was the only Canadian prime minister who ever went to a foreign war. During all his years as a civil servant and as a politician he made sure that no one tried to call him a war hero or even mentioned his service. He did have a little drink with an ambassador from time to time, some red wine from France, for example. When he wanted to cross Wellington Street to get to his place of work, he looked both ways in the Ottawa sunlight.

STAIRCASE DESCENDED

I opened my eyes or I open my eyes and thought or think it was or is morning. That is a terrible sentence to begin with. I take it back. I open my eyes, usually, and think it might be morning. How do you know? Your, no, my glasses are on the top of the bookcase and so is the clock with its red numerals and they tell the time. But can they be said to tell the time if there is no one in the room who is capable of reading the numerals? That is not the kind of question one, yes that's a good one, one—one wants to ask or even answer first thing in the morning. If it is morning.

One wants to stay in bed, of course, and to hell with the time of day. But one is also predisposed to getting out of bed. For me that is a problem, the first one of the probable day. Here is the problem: when I wake up I am lying on my right side, knees as close to my chest as possible, one hand under the pillow or rather my head because the pillow has fallen to the floor, there is no pillow. The other hand, who knows? It could be pulled up under my chin. My knees as close to my chest as possible. When I was young, I could tuck my knees right up against my chest. No more. But of all the things I cannot make my body do any more, this business with the knees is the least of my troubles. I can lift the knees a lot closer than most men or even women my age, I will wager.

The problem is getting my body out of bed. I do not mean a slacking of the will. I mean that when I wake, nearly blind eyes looking at a red blur of unknown numerals, my body is locked in that position I was so careful to describe just a moment ago. And mind you, I am sick and tired of description. If I go on with this, I might have some difficulty with description. I might not do it. You will not find me throwing around adjectives, in any case. I hate the goddamned slithery unnecessary corruptive willful Anglo-Saxon self-satisfied secondary stylish things. Ha, just a little joke there, you don't mind? To hell with you, too. Just fooling.

Trying to get that body out of that bed. It might help if I described the bed, but I won't. The body is locked in place by a small imperfection low down in the vertebraic column. If the body lies in roughly the same position for a given period of time, as for instance when I am asleep, it is next to impossible to change its attitude. For instance, I cannot induce it to lie on its back and stretch its legs straight toward the so-called foot of the bed. Nor can I swing the legs over the side of the bed, though my body lies on the edge, not the middle of the bed. It is a medium-wide bed. My father died in it, and there was a woman who used to find room for her body beside mine. In those days my body did not lie in the same position all night.

Many people get out of bed by swinging their legs together, rotating on their buttocks, perhaps, and allowing their trunks to be levered to a vertical position as their heels fall to the floor, where there may be cold wood or gritty linoleum or a warm wool carpet. A warm wool carpet. If there were a warm wool carpet in this room, I might sleep on it and avoid this problem of getting out of the bed. But then the problem of rising vertical from the carpet might be even more daunting. I return to the appropriate problem. I wished and I wish that I could rotate and rise, my heels falling on whatever is down there, sometimes it is hard to remember all these things. That is connected to my dislike of description, I am sure. If I find that I cannot remember something that one would never imagine forgetting, anyone's forgetting, one wants to crawl under the covers if he can find them, and go back to sleep, if you can call what I do sleeping.

Not that I don't try the various ways of getting up in the morning. It is impossible, thank goodness, to describe the feeling when one wants to get up but the body will not do it. It is not the same thing as wanting to move your arm when you wake up with your arm asleep over your head. You begin to move your left leg, let us say, and a signal arrives saying that you will soon be in great familiar pain without hope of gaining some movement at its cost. Hopeless. The signal comes from the small place in the lower region of the sacroiliac, you remember that word. It was very popular in radio show jokes in the late forties.

So here is what I do—I could list all the ways I fail every morning, but I cannot summon the energy to try to remember them, and if I miss out a few I will not be proud enough of my list, knowing that you will then think that things are not really as bad as all that. Well, why should I care about that? It is too late now, anyway. Here is what I wind up doing. With extremely small movements I nudge the body closer to the edge of the bed. This nudging is meticulous and painstaking and would seem to be hopeless of success if I had not done it on previous occasions. First I might point the big toe on my top, that is left, foot toward the bookcase and move the foot a bit. Then the lower or right shoulder. Then, with the long bony loose-skinned fingers, damned description, of both hands wrapped around the corner of the edge of the mattress, I manage to bounce the round bony ball of my right hip an inch, or is it a centimetre, over, to the right, that is. You will just have to imagine, if you can summon your faculties better than I can mine, how long this procedure goes on and with what discomfort I must continue it. It makes my body sweat, which is amusing, because my body affords a comparison with the denuded skin of a mature chicken, and one has never seen a chicken perspire, no matter what other discomfiting things one has seen a chicken do. Sweating like that every morning or whenever it is I get out of bed, and, yes, I finally do, I wish momentarily for a shower. Place of potential disaster. Enough, and more.

Enough. If I do not get at it I will never tell you how I get out of bed and thus solve the first problem of the day. And why

bother getting up, you ask. I do not get up. After enough
edging and pointing and minute hopping with my frozen shut
body, I manage to propel myself so far to my right that I
achieve the edge and more of the bed. Of course I have not
been able to rotate on my hips as we would all like to, but I do
turn as I depart the bed, and fall face downward to the floor.
There is no stopping me then, not till I come to rest on whatever that surface is. Of course, I always remember if I am
jolted enough. It is hardwood, nice dark boards of hardwood.
Once they shone, a rich dark brown lateral glint of—no. There
is a bang, of course, when I cease falling, and even though I
have my hands in position to prevent my face from striking the
hardwood, I do land nice and crisp on my knees and elbows,
and so the tight grip thus far maintained by the little spot of
imperfection in my vertebraic column is slackened just a little.
Enough so that in my present position I can begin a careful
crawl toward the toilet.

2

Sometimes it is a crawl and sometimes it is more like a creep,
a creeping, let us say, to avoid vulgar ambiguity. It would be
nice just to stand up and walk or at least hobble to the bathroom, and on the odd occasion I can do just that, if on the route
there are enough objects or close enough walls I fall into so
that I can support myself on something. There are times when
I start by standing up, having pulled myself up the brass leg of
the bed, but have to collapse to the hardwood again because

the first step or shuffle, let us say, brings a serrated knife blade, this is a fanciful description, you understand, into the small of my back. A small that is the largest thing in my attention at the time. Poor jest, but necessary.

I proceed, embarrassed a little, I mean here is a grown, perhaps, man, on his hand and knees (if it is one of my lucky mornings) crawling out of his bedroom into the hallway and, turning a little to the left, into the bathroom. If you are a man, or if at least a man a little like me, you know that in the morning there is a compulsion you cannot shake. In fact it is often the agent that gets you out of bed in the first place. This is the unnegotiable necessity of passing water. Some people are lucky: they hop out of bed in the morning, perhaps flinging their arms wide of their trunks in a little reminder of elementary-school exercises, and hippity hop to the toilet, where they pull it out and piddle away, great creamy suds rising on the sides of the bowl, a 1950s radio song humming in their heads.

While I am crawling toward the bathroom and then across the bathroom to the convenience, fifteen men in my neighbourhood have done just what I outlined above. I crawl past the sink, along the flank of the bathtub, noticing for the hundredth time that one of its clawed feet has a smear of toothpaste on it, and how did that get there again? It could not, certainly, be the same smear that was there, let us say, last February the twelfth. But there I am then at the device. There is a certain principle at work now—the more movement I am capable of, the more I am capable of movement. It is as though the knot in my back is melting. In an hour or so I will be walking like a normal man or a normal man with a body made of shredded wheat, as I once quipped to Marsha, a woman you will never hear about again. Here I am. But there is no question of waiting until I can perambulate. Not that it is not a temptation. Just let the bladder go, let it unblad, I suppose you could say, and relax. Reeelaaax, says the voice in my left ear. That is where the devil sits when he has time, my mother once said. Enough about her. There will be no resorting to "motivation" in this account.

There I am. There is no question, then, of pointing Percy at the porcelain. I am committed, you might say if this were more serious, this telling, to telling you the details. The truth is that I could stop right here, and I would not mind. You would probably cheer the abandonment. In fact it is unlikely that you have made it this far. If you have, please sign your initials right here: . All right, there I am. I am 186 centimetres in height on the occasions when I can stand up fully. I have never been able to measure the toilet bowl in centimetres, but it is just under fourteen inches in height. All right, I will just tell you and let's forget it. I kneel full of gratitude that I am there and hang poor Percy over the hard white lip. On most occasions he has reached by now the condition of hangability. But there are mornings on which he will not retreat from the condition he was found to be in on my waking. I do not know or have forgotten what those neighbours of mine do on such an occasion, but I can tell you what I do. I can tell you but just this once I do not believe that I will.

Flushed not too far from my embarrassed face, the toilet is
finished for now, and glad I am of it. Now there is the sink and
perhaps the shower. I would like to take a shower every
morning. In fact there was a time a few years back when I did,
and not always alone, I can tell you. What a ridiculous image,
you say. All right then, you will get urine and atrocious posture
instead of soapy euripus. Now I simply hope that by the time
I am ready for the shower I can stand up in it. There is nothing
gratifying about coming to rest on one's hands and knees in the
tub and feeling the hard water against one's back. But first the
sink. I always feel a little guilty when it comes to the sink. This
guilt reaches, as most do, a long way back, into childhood,
when one's mother warned one about putting one's weight on
the poor sink. Damn. There is something about a bathroom
that allows one's mother to sidle into the discussion, the mono-
logue, yes, I know. But you are here, aren't you, you did sign
in, didn't you?

All right, I pull myself up the sink, like a sickly monkey
pulling himself up the bars that imprison him while offering
him something to ascend. There you go, a simile, I think. You
will not, if I have my wits about me, see another of those. Bad
enough that I fell into this so-called present tense. No, I made
a promise to myself not to spend all my precious time talking
about this talking. If it is talking. It looks more like writing to
me. There I go. Okay, a short paragraph. I decided on para-
graphs, with you in mind. You might remember that.

Up the sink I climbed. (That felt good. Not the climbing. I
mean the tense.) (This will get out of hand. I really must stop

that sort of thing right now, no matter what attractive thoughts
come to mind.) By now I can bear this, the simulacrum of
standing while leaning heavily on the basin. I can manage to
get the stopper in. I didn't use one for years till I started paying
for my own hot water. The taps on. The object is to wash and
then debarbarate the face. Now my 186 centimetres give me a
new problem, or rather the revisiting of an old problem. I
cannot bend to get my face anywhere near the right altitude for
laving. I must spread my feet as far apart as possible, rest my
bony forearms on the edge of the porcelain, and do the best I
can, bobbing my head for a painful half-second, and throwing
water and soap toward my cheeks. This goes on. I want to stop
but I have to proceed. I want to stop writing or talking or thinking, but you cannot. You cannot stop thinking if you are not a
Himalayan anchorite, and what else is there? So, eventually one
gets a razor in one's hand and eventually manages to make
momentary scrapes at the face. It is a little like reaching for a
piece of paper that is just out of reach on the floor on the other
side of those monkey bars. If you overextend your shoulder and
elbow and wrist for a second before they all snap back into their
proper proportions, you can make a little scrape at the whiskers
and soap if you have the razor at the correct angle. This is how
I shave almost every morning. I have thought of growing a
beard but I cannot. I have random hairs on my face, no pattern
and certainly no carpet. I used to tell myself that this unmanli-
ness was a sign that I was a forerunner of human beings from
the future. I read a lot of science fiction in my youth, and time
travel was my favourite narrative device. I was going to say

something about that but I cannot remember what it was. Let us say that I have shaved.

Perhaps now I can get into the shower. The main reasons one gets into the shower, or the main reasons I do, are my hair and the cleft between my buttocks. Perhaps I can get into the shower and at least lean against the wall.

3

Now we come to the heart of this story. It is a story, don't you agree? Now we come to what I thought of as the whole of the story. I could probably put this a better way if I started all over again. But then what would you have? Probably a well-rehearsed narrative and therefore something you cannot trust. If you think that is literary theory, think again. There is nothing at all literary here, I the least so.

I am now approaching the bottom of the stairs from above. That is, I am descending. Not at all like the royalty those words might make one think of. I am wearing a pair of slippers so old that I can't remember who gave them to me. One never buys one's own slippers any more than one buys one's own after-shave lotion. They, the slippers, have heels that have been crushed under my own for so long that they would appear to someone who has not yet put on his glasses for the day to be made that way. There are plenty of slippers with no backs to them, you know that. You also know by now that I am for some reason slow to get to this heart of the story I promised or at least mentioned. I am also, I must tell you, since I started on this dressing of the narrator, wearing my ratty old bathrobe, or is it housecoat? It is an item that falls to a level just below my knees and is belted at approximately the waist. That is all. Under this piece of drab phlegm-green terry cloth I am as naked and as attractive as a hog hanging in the cold room at Peerless Packers.

Ah, say you, ablutions done and staircase descended, he is now going to perform the comfortably familiar ritual of the morning newspaper and fresh egg. That is, ah, say you, all this while at the same time saying it looks as if this person is going to force upon me or us a lot more sentences than we need about every moment of his waking and God help us perhaps sleeping life. Not so. At least I hope not so: I did not, I will admit, plan on narrating the getting down out of bed and the getting up to the white bowls. How about this: I think that you can depend on my torpor to protect you from a recounting in the familiar present tense of my whole day, one like the next that they are.

No, this is the point at which you encounter not a fresh egg and a minimal daily, but two women at a kitchen table, drinkers of so much coffee that in an hour they will be taking turns at the downstairs toilet, and expenders of more words in that hour than appear in the missing newspaper. It is not really missing, save from this account. Either it is on the front steps where it has been for five hours, or some child, pauper, or dog has made off with it again. If there has been a high wind earlier this morning, its pages will be wet to transparency and wrapped around various bushes or weeds in the yard and the neighbour's yard. The neighbour does not read the newspaper. He is a longhaired youth whose occupation seems to be burglary, judging from the peculiar coming and going of packing cases and trailing electrical cords. But you will not be bothered with him again. I do not even know his name, so I can not even withhold that from you.

So to those two women sitting at the kitchen table, the way women will, sprawling a little, no, that is not quite right, their bodies relaxed so much that they seem to be saying with their easeful slouch that they own the space. No, I will never get that right, so I will drop the attempt. One might as well commit a lot of description, or lay out a row of similes. Anyway, there they are, the two of them, total weight, let us say of 150 kilograms, maybe less. The prettier one is the neighbour lady, but the other one is smarter. She is the one who is related to me by marriage. She thinks that I am gone, and she has her friend persuaded of that illusion. Sometimes it sounds to me as if she thinks that I am dead and gone; other times it seems as if she is convinced that I am just gone, fled, fallen away. Just disappeared from sight. I do not do everything I could do to persuade her otherwise, but I make small attempts in that direction. Why do people call that a direction? Let it stand. I hardly can myself.

They are having one of their usual discussions. This is what the lady of the house says:

"Each thing itself, then, and its essence are one and the same in no merely accidental way, as is evident both from the preceding arguments and because to *know* each thing, at least, is just to know its essence, so that even by the exhibition of instances it becomes clear that both must be one."

To which her visitor responds:

"Ha ha ha ha. You may be right about that and you may be wrong. You could not prove it by me. All I know is that when my old man wants what he wants and I don't want what he wants, essence, well, essence never enters into it. It might have worked differently for you when your old man was around. Might have been essence all over the place. Ha ha ha ha. Far as I know. Ho ho."

Now the woman who lives in this house never condescends to her friends or any stranger. She just assumes that they enjoy the possibility of entering the conversation, when they get the chance to talk, at a level that will be commensurate, is that a usable word here, with the one she is speaking on. So she will continue (ah, the future tense, which no more covers the future than the present tense the present):

"For it has been already shown that the soul of the incarnate deity is often supposed to transmigrate at death into another incarnation; and if this takes place when the death is a natural one, there seems no reason why it should not take place when the death has been brought about by violence. Certainly the idea that the soul of a dying person may be transmitted to his successor is perfectly familiar to primitive peoples."

"I wish I had known that yesterday when I was at the houseplant sale at Corby's," says her fellow coffee-drinker. "That place was full of primitive people yesterday. Oh my!"

At this juncture I decide to try to make my presence known. Luckily, I *have* had a shower this late morning, and that stream of hot, nearly steaming water on the small of my back makes it possible for me to walk, even on a level surface. I generally start with a significant stare at one of the two women. Sometimes the visitor is not there; on that occasion I stare at my close relative, bending my neck down the way a pigeon does when it is contemplating a puddle but wary of a crowd of human feet. Having inaugurated the stare, I lift my left hand to a level with my left nipple, wrist tucked in to trunk, and wiggle the upward pointing fingers a little. When you do that, trying to make each digit independent of the others, the middle finger, the longest, usually refrains from wiggling. Nevertheless, I hope that it *appears* to be wiggling because its neighbours are so doing. I do not want to be thought to be disguising a rude gesture, even with the palm facing the wrong way. Not yet, in any case.

"There is an unmistakable indication in the text of Sophocles' tragedy itself that the legend of Oedipus sprang from some primeval dream-material that had as its content the distressing disturbance of a child's relation to his parents owing to the first stirrings of sexuality."

"Stirrings!" exclaimed the neighbour. "It's too bad you never had any children before he departed. My boys are stirring all the time. I tell you I hate cleaning up their room. And sometimes I don't feel at all safe myself!"

You could not say the word "sexuality" to this woman without rousing her. Even sitting still in her chair, forearms on the table between them, she seemed to experience a sea change. Her body seemed to become more rounded, to make rounded areas of shininess in her print dress. Perspiration made her throat glow, and moisture appeared in the edges of hair over her ear. Her mouth would not entirely close when it was relieved of its labour of speech. Moisture shone from her front teeth. Her eyes, which before had been simply brown and cool, now glowed as if all at once connected to the electrical power lying patiently in the wires inside the walls between rooms. The palms of her hands were probably wet. The creases at the backs of her knees were likely sticky. She moved her knees a little farther apart, looking, in all likelihood, for air.

How disappointing. I had intended, as you will have gathered, to spare you that sort of thing. The foregoing description should appear thus:

~~You could not say the word "sexuality" to this woman without rousing her. Even sitting still in her chair, forearms on the table between them, she seemed to experience a sea change. Her body seemed to become more rounded, to make rounded areas of shininess in her print dress. Perspiration made her throat glow, and moisture appeared in the edges of hair over her ear. Her mouth would not entirely close when it was relieved of its labour of speech. Moisture shone from her front teeth. Her eyes, which before had been simply brown and cool, now glowed as if all at once connected to the electrical power lying patiently in the wires inside the walls between rooms. The palms of her hands were probably wet. The creases at the backs of her knees were likely sticky. She~~

~~moved her knees a little farther apart, looking, in all likeli-~~
~~hood, for air.~~

You think that you know what you would do in this situation? You have that profound confidence? The universe for
you is not a maze with possible beasts at the end of any
corridor? I congratulate you on your good fortune. I am without
envy. I simply wish to express my joy that there is such a
fortunate one among us, and therefore maybe many. Joy is
likely too exalted a word. What can I put in its place? I suppose
we could agree on satisfaction. All right, my satisfaction. But
now you must also allow that it is not for me a simple decision
to say or do what I do or did in the above circumstance.

I am not stupid: I know that you are objecting to my silence
here. Why, you ask, do I not shout at the women to make them
notice and indeed acknowledge my existence and more than
that my presence? And while we are at it, why do I not effect
another conducting of the senses; that is, why do I or did I not
reach out and touch the woman of my choice here? Why not
grasp the neighbour lady's thigh or seize a handful of my
matrimonial partner's raven hair and pull it, vertically or hori-
zontally about seven centimetres, or to be more certain,
fifteen? I do not know whether I will be able to explain this to
you. I know that there must be personalities like mine in the
world, personalities that have been shaped more or less like
mine over all the years of our growing up, albeit like potatoes
growing in rocky soil, some of us being compelled to grow
around a rock and never to achieve the shape assigned to the
potato in the little golden book of west coast gardening. If you

happen to be one of those rare but surely extant personalities, you will understand easily why I did not make those auditory or palpatory attempts at communication. In fact it is probable that I would not have to waste breath or ink or whatever I am expending in the explanation. You would intuit and agree, you would find the parallel in or behind your meek heart. For the others, probably the majority of you, I can try the outline of an explanation. Probably anyone, of any personality, will have a layer, a striation of my condition, if condition is an appropriate word here, and I am reluctant to admit it.

All right, for you, the majority, I will try this. If I were to reach out and touch or grab or caress or pull, whether the pretty one or the smart one, and if I could feel the touch and the recipient could not, I would be, ontologically speaking, in trouble. If she could feel it and I could not, I would be filled with doubt at best. If neither of us could feel it—that is, if my hand went right through, say, the upper leg of the woman from down the street, it could mean any number of things. It could mean that we are both goners or creatures of the imagination, and if so, whose? It could mean that I am dreaming, or at least that one of us is, or if that is not stretching likelihood too far, both of us are. It could be that we are both figures in a fiction whose perpetrator is not paying sufficient attention for the moment. It could mean that this is the general rule of things and that my long-held opinion that matter comes to rest against the surface of matter is in error. The possibilities are not endless, but the end is too far away for the amount of energy I have to spare for postulating its place.

Suffice it to say that I am aware of many possibilities that I do not want to prove or have proven for me.

It would be a simple thing to attempt a casual, accidental-seeming touch, if there were not other hints of my non-existence, at least as far as these women and the dimension they were in was concerned; and here I go into some sort of past tense again. If they acknowledged me by sight, and were not just ignoring me but unaware of my being, I could touch them without any but the normal fears, a knuckle to the temple or whatever. But then the touch would be unnecessary, as this explanation would be were I speaking or writing to people who could easily understand my attitude. But because these people seemed not to be able to notice me (and this is not just a singular instance, you must remember) by sight, there was a good chance that they would not notice me by touch because the latter was impossible. If not a good chance, at least a chance. As it is, at least till the present time, I would rather try another time to make them notice me by sight, just *in case* they were ignoring me out of spite. I want to hold onto the illusion, if it is an illusion, that I exist, for a while.

There was another possible explanation that I was going to offer, but now I feel that it would take a considerable feat of memory and thought to bring it to the surface of my brain, and I would rather return now to the narrative, if you will agree that that is what I departed from. Besides, the explanation, for those of you who do not resemble me in the most particular of my traits, would be overlong. It is likely that I would lose you, either in the sentences or from the room.

In the meantime, if that is not a silly thing to say at the preface of this resumption, I am in that other room, let us call it a living room—requisite number of furniture items, crooked magazines on one of them, and I can see the brace of women through the extra-wide kitchen door, at least it is the kitchen door from my viewpoint. From theirs it is probably the living room door. It is not really a door, but rather a kind of formality for those who like to know that they are passing between rooms, a kind of minimal archway, really a rounding of the corners, a sort of slight decrease in the distance from wall to wall. Through this thing I will call a door simply for the sake of this narrative, which I persist in misnaming it, I can see the two women and hear their conversation as suggested above. I mean I don't expect you to believe that I have caught a verbatim series of remarks from one particular afternoon—I am using the present tense from time to time, after all. Really I just went and selected some likely passages from books of an unmistakably intellectual bent.

Now what I do is to remove my clothes. I cannot remember what I said I was wearing, so I will rely on you to remember, or to go back and look it up. Let us say that I was wearing pajamas, my ratty old striped blue-and-white ones that I have to hold the pants of up unless I am wearing my old greenish terry cloth robe. Well, let us say, or I will, that I was at the moment in question wearing all that stuff. And my bedroom slippers, the ones, I remember now, with the squashed down heels. I take all these things off. No, I don't. But I undo the belt of my robe, and then I let the pajama bottoms drop. I kick off my bedroom slippers in order to kick off the pajama bottoms that have settled around my feet. Then I can dance.

Here is what the dance looks like. Rather, here is what I imagine the dance to look like; as the dancer I am in no position to observe or reflect on the dance. I hold the skirts of my off-green terry cloth robe in my two hands and lift them sideways, away from my body. Then I contrive to bend my bony legs, knobby, really, they are knobby at the hip, knee, ankle, and foot, bend my knobby legs and kick my feet out sideways. All this time I make certain that I am facing the conversation at the kitchen table. I might describe an arc, little part of a semi-circle, there in the adjoining room, but always with the effect of total angular continuity. I dance and dance. I take a chance and kick my bony heel knobs together. My genitals swing back and forth in opposition to my legs. That is, when my legs are kicking left, my genitals are still swinging right. But enough about them. I don't think that my genitals are any funnier or any more an affront than the rest of my white, hairless, smooth, gravity-formed body.

What do I want? Do I want to test the limits of their ability to pretend that I am not there? Am I by now allowing that I might not exist, at least for them, and enjoying a dare otherwise prevented by childhood training in repression and civility? Why don't I approach, why don't I press the advantage that would be granted by proximity? I believe that I have explained that above, at least for those readers or listeners who would benefit by explanation, that is, understand and even, perhaps, sympathize. Now, wouldn't that be grand? Sympathy.

I, even were I not after all a literary figure, as I am sure I am for you, one that you may even have grown tired of, would appreciate and welcome sympathy as quickly as the next fellow. But now I was finding it to be as much as I could handle to try for recognition.

How did my audience, if I may have your indulgence in calling them that for the nonce, react to my terpsichorean antics? After I had exhausted myself, and was sprawled out in what had been her father's favourite easy chair, legs extended in front of me, skirts of my robe falling behind each stringy thigh, this is what I heard them to say:

"Diogenes, another follower of Anaximenes, held that air was the ultimate element of all things, but that nothing could be produced from it without the agency of the divine reason, which permeated it. Anaxagoras was followed by his pupil Archelaus. He, too, asserted that everything in the universe was composed of like particles, which, however, were informed by intelligence. This mind, by causing the conjunction and disso-lution of the eternal bodies or particles, was the source of all movements."

"I'd have to think for a while to agree about *all movements*. I got a husband, and you don't know how lucky you are some-times, and two huge boys, and I can't believe that there is any mind behind their movements, especially when they are coming down the stairs or when they are picking up knives and forks, when I can convince them to use such elementary tools."

I was exhausted. There was nothing more I could do there. I was certainly not going to go into the kitchen to get coffee or a muffin or even a piece of limp broccoli. I did not want to play ghost, because I might start to believe in my own demise. I did not want to touch one of those people. What if I touched one, and she responded in such a way as to show that she had known I was there all the time? One does not like to entertain the notion that one is that little worthy of remark. I would go upstairs, and then I would decide whether to get dressed and go out, thinking of the near impossibility of donning socks, of bending to stick one over a big toe, and if I did go out I would get a cup of coffee and even a lemon-guck-filled Danish pastry. I would go to Daphne's Lunch. Everyone knows me there. They say hello and say my name out loud when I enter the premises. They know enough to let me sit at a banquette even when I am using a table for four, because of my bad back. I am visible there. I do not know the names of any of the waitresses or the regular patrons I see there every time I attend. But we are a community. A community of laggards, perhaps, but a polis.

4

Perhaps you will agree that that scene, with the two talkative women and the dancing geezer, was the heart of this story, given that you have already acceded to the notion that this is a story. What, then, will we call the following? The following scene, perhaps a kind of loosening of the knot we have got ourselves tied in, takes place in Daphne's Lunch, where you will not hear saints and thinkers discussed all that often. Oh, once in a while I will quote Heraclitus to some hapless toiler for the minimum wage. But in general, philosophy is not broached there. Until today. Or that day. Let us say today.

Today I found myself talking with an old gent who seemed to admire his ability to pick a tea bag out of its cup and suspend it over its home in such a way that the drips of tea will fall into the centre of the red-brown liquid. No, I *find* myself talking with him. I do not know his name, and I do not think that he knows mine. It is in such circumstances that one may find oneself these days. There is a little ambiguity for you, I mean that sentence. But you knew that, didn't you? All right, I will get on with this tale. Nice day. Nice day. Haven't seen such nice weather this time of year in years. Last year we were soaking wet and cold as hell this time of year. This kind of weather is good for your rheumatism. Good for what ails you. You bet. Wouldn't mind being thirty years younger all the same. You bet, I would settle for twenty.

And so on. I know how to tailor my conversation for this crowd. It never strikes me that the guy I am talking with might be tailoring his conversation for this crowd, with me as part of this crowd. Who knows? We may, if we were to meet somewhere else, say one of the conference rooms at the Regency Hotel, have begun a discussion of Anaxagoras and his tradition. Be that as it may, we got onto a discussion of ontology or the like anyway. How we got there from the quite ordinary weather, I do not recall. Or I do not want to write or say it out. Eventually I got most of the lemon guck into my mouth and some on my lap, and was in conversation. I could end this account right here, and not make it any the less inconclusive than it is going to be. You will say that you would have liked to be warned of that at least around page four. Well, here is your chance. You can drop it right now, leave the beanery, browse the bookstore, two blocks east, cross the street, find an uplifting story or a meaningful fiction. Let me suggest the paperback edition of Michael Ondaatje's *Running in the Family*. Even if you don't buy it, you will have avoided the following conversation:

"My wife can't see me."

"You too?"

"She looks right through me."

"They are like that. That is why they are wives."

I let him sip his tea. I allowed the waitress to refill my coffee cup. I had to think about this. How will I relate to this gent who doubtless has a name but one that does not hang in the air between us, a story that will not be instantly convertible into the clichés of figurative language surrounding connubial friction?

"She thinks that I am dead. Or if not that, she is of the opinion that I have in some less mortal way retired from the site of our domicile. She thinks that I am no longer there."

"Sounds just like my wife, bless her departed soul."

Back there, I think, in the heart of the story, I cannot persuade anyone of my existence, much less my propinquity. Now my appearance, in such an habitual location, is unquestioned. I can now not speak the opposite. I can't persuade someone of my absence, my non-being, albeit only in the eyes, or rather out of the eyes and mind of another, or in this case two others, at least.

It strikes me that this gent without the name may think that he is only speaking with a reverie, only imagining this conversation, imagining that there is a coffee-drinking fellow with a bad back with whom he is in conversation. It is late morning. Old bones rest and old brains enjoy their little trips.

"Have a look at me," I say.

People don't, as a rule, like to do that in places like Daphne's. They usually let their eyes flit. To the waitress as she turns her back and carries something to the kitchen hole. To the passing balloon outside the window, a kid has been to a celebrating bank. To the widow at another table. She is smoking a cigarette and reading a small paperback novel placed inside a leatherette cover. But this fellow does look now.

"Am I to look at anything in particular?" he says.

"Can you see a scar on my face?"

He looks.

"Yes I can."

"Where is it?"

"Well, there are two. There is a small one right at your hairline above the middle of your forehead, and there is a slightly longer one that runs from the corner of your mouth down at a 45-degree angle."

It was more like a 30-degree angle, but I let it go.

"Thank you."

All right, I do exist. At least in this circumstance, in this environment, I exist.

"So to you I am visible," I suggest.

"Sure. Unless you are not supposed to be here. If your wife calls, I will say I haven't seen you, if you want."

"No, no. That's not what I mean. She would never phone this place anyway. Nor would she enter it willingly. She goes to well-lit places where they serve little things on croissants for seven dollars."

All right, I have settled the question of whether he is imagining me. There is still the question about whether I have created him. If he is a product of my imagination, there is not all that much currency in his attestation that he can see me as well as talk with me.

It strikes me that I could just rest comfortable, take everything at face value. But is also strikes me that I am not any better off than I was in the living room of my own house, except that here I am enjoying a second cup of coffee. There I was pretty well convinced of my presence; I was propiocepting quite handily, thank you. But others were not reflecting knowledge and awareness of my corporeal entity. Here I receive outside attestation of my being and presence, but I feel the possibility of uncertainty as to whether I have not generated, mentally, of course, the agent of that corroboration.

I should, perhaps, as they say, have stood in bed.

Maybe I did. But no, I cannot accept that. I cannot allow that all that pain of rising for the dubious day was nothing, or for nothing. Or that it will be if I do it. I do not want to spend a life made from now on and who knows how long till now, made entirely of mentation. Of course all you can receive

through the agency of this expenditure of words is something
that resembles mentation more than it does any more physical
and palpable action, if we can speak of action rather than the
thing acting as palpable. Maybe I don't even palpate anything
any more. Did I just imagine being downstairs and dancing?
Am I not now sitting on a reddish banquette at Daphne's,
thinking of my hard bed as down that street, up those stairs? Is
there anyone reading or hearing this?

THE OUTHOUSE

W hen Bob Small and I were kids, we liked going to the Lawrence Theatre to see Red Skelton movies and Bob Hope movies. We knew in our hearts that these two great men would become our role models. But Randolph Scott is the greatest movie actor of all time! It was during this Lawrence Theatre Saturday afternoon era that I really got into Hollywood musicals. I am not interested now in *Les Miz* or *Cats* or any of that stuff, but I really liked those Howard Keel films.

No one ever threw anything in the Lawrence Theatre. The presence of Mr. Gough was enough to make us behave. Actually, we were a well-behaved generation in Lawrence in those days. Except the time I fell into the outhouse hole.

—Hey, Small, would I be doing my reputation any good by telling the behaviour-deity this story? Please advise.

—C'mon, you know you can't resist telling the story, but I'll bet you leave all my heroic efforts to save you out of it.

—Bobbo, that happened before I knew you, when I was in grade four and living at Katie's place. Do you want the behaviour-deity to think our stories are unreliable?

—Oh, I thought it happened when Mr. Laird wouldn't give us anything when we were trick-or-treating, but maybe that was just a come-to-think-of-it.

—That was just a come-to-think-of-it. You know, I think that usually outhouse holes are full of piled shit and flies and torn bits of catalogue. But this one was wet.

Well, Katie was Katie Rindisbacher, a beautiful brunette who wore pleated plaid skirts and saddle oxfords and bobby sox. We lived in a house that was in her father's orchard, and I spent a lot of time with Katie and her friend Sylvia MacNab.

Sylvia MacNab asked me to the Sadie Hawkins dance in grade nine, but I always thought it was just out of sympathy for me and my awkward trying to come to terms with a hopeless love for her. But now I think, fifty years later, What if she really liked me and wanted this relationship to blossom?

—But, Dels, you never showed such sensitivity at the time. You told me she had the hots for you, and that I would never learn to handle broads nearly as adroitly as you. You said some guys just got it and some don't. But I did okay. While you were at the dance with Sylvia I was across the border in Oroville, where I almost had to beat them off with a stick when I asked, "Hoos aboot it?"

Well, years later, when there was the twentieth-year reunion of my graduating class, I was all excited because I hadn't heard from or about Sylvia MacNab for twenty years, and she didn't show. I found out from the paper they sent around that she lived in New Westminster and had several kids.

Okay, to get back to the topic—well, it was, of course, traditional, in the literature, that kids do certain things on Halloween: soap windows, steal front gates, push over outhouses. The outhouse in question on Halloween, 1944, was on a rise of dry land that rose up out of Mr. Rindisbacher's orchard, a little north and west of our house. Leonard Kovak lived down a dirt road that went east of this outhouse. I can't remember any house nearby, so that is a little vague in my memory. That is, the terrain outside the outhouse hole's perimeter is somewhat vague to my recall.

I am pretty sure Leonard Kovak was one of the other outhouse pushers. There were, I think, four of us. We were in grade four, and I got the impression that these guys did this sort of stuff all the time, like the guys in stories and so on. I had been in Lawrence for only a year and a bit, so I was still learning to socialize, though I think I remember that there were times when I was a class show-off smart aleck, maybe.

Still, in addition to being a class cut-up I was also a little Jansenite boy, or at least so some Catholic kid called me, and so I had all this strict private morality, all about how I should not smoke or drink or deprive Maureen of her virginity, no matter how understanding she might be about it. So I was the kind of kid who would repair things rather than wrecking them on Halloween, and it was very odd that I should have been there, pushing on the side of that outhouse in the dark.

Leonard Kovak kept surprising me. I was surprised when he became a terrific athlete, and we were then supposed to call him Len. I was surprised when he started going steady with Joan Williams (the Student Body), and then years later I was surprised when he became a high-school teacher in the Cariboo, and then I was really surprised when he became the teacher in charge of the student drama actors in his school. Amazing, every one of those moves.

So there I was with my newish Lawrence rural friends, pushing over the outhouse, just as in the books and comic books and legends and all. Soon three of those guys would be gone in the night, while I remained *in situ*. Now here there was no chance of explaining to Bob Small what I explained when I showed up where he didn't expect me, in the old Boy Scout Hall grounds. . . .

So what I am saying is: I had this personal Jansenist loathing of the idea of outhouse toppling, but I also yearned to make steady friends of my peers. It was a dilemma. Later, of course, I would see my fate as a punishment for going with the peers instead of sticking to my personal superior morality. . . .

Yeah, so that it becomes odd to imagine Len Kovak being a kid who would push over an outhouse. Although it must seem even stranger to think of me being such a kid, except for those blighted minds who think my genius rebellion was allied to juvenile delinquency. I wasn't thinking of that, of course, when I realized how hard it was going to be to get out of that wet hole without help.

So what could I say, but that I was a regular guy. So we rocked and pushed, and the thing came down easier than I had thought it would, among the cactus and couch grass and sage-brush and tumbleweed. Down it came, and of course it was my luck that it went over so fast that I was still pushing when there was nothing to push but air, dark fetid air with a trace of lime dust.

Now, I have looked in a lot of outhouse holes, I mean through the hole, downward, and they usually contain a mound of pretty solid shit of every hue, mixed with various kinds of paper. One would think that these things are pretty well standard.

Well, it was really hard to get out of that hole. But I came out the bottom with my rubber boots on. That was a lie I told Bob Small on any given occasion.

Okay, Mum, is that a story?

acknowledgments

"At the Store" was published in *Prairie Fire*, autumn 2000, vol. 21, no. 3.

"Carter Fell," "Old Bottles," and "A Short Story" were published in *A Place to Die*, Oberon Press, 1983.

"The Creator Has a Master Plan" was published in *Protective Footwear*, McClelland & Stewart, 1978.

"The Elevator" and "How Delsing Met Francis and Started to Write a Novel" were published in *Flycatcher & Other Stories*, Oberon Press, 1974.

"Joining the Lost Generation" was a chapbook published by House Press, 2002.

"Little Me," "Rhode Island Red," and "Staircase Descended" were published in *The Rain Barrel* © Talonbooks, Vancouver, 1994.

"The Outhouse" was published in *New Quarterly*, spring 2003, no. 86

"Pretty as a Picture" was published in *Border/Lines*, 1997, no. 44.

"Standing on Richards" was published in *The Malahat Review*, fall 2000, no. 132, and in *Best Canadian Stories 01*, edited by Douglas Glover, Oberon Press, 2001.

"Two Glasses of Remy" was published in *The Capilano Review*, fall 1999, vol. 2, no. 29.